Hidden Evil

Karen Brady

Contents

Disclaimer	vii
Dubai – Present Day	xi
Chapter 1	1
Chapter 2	5
Chapter 3	11
Chapter 4	15
Chapter 5	23
Chapter 6	25
Chapter 7	29
Chapter 8	37
Chapter 9	43
Chapter 10	49
Chapter 11	53
Chapter 12	61
Chapter 13	65
Chapter 14	67
Chapter 15	71
Chapter 16	77
Chapter 17	81
Chapter 18	89
Chapter 19	93
Chapter 20	105
Chapter 21	111
Chapter 22	117
Chapter 23	123
Chapter 24	127
Chapter 25	133
Chapter 26	137

Chapter 27	145
Chapter 28	153
Chapter 29	165
Chapter 30	171
Chapter 31	175
Chapter 32	179
Chapter 33	183
Chapter 34	187
Chapter 35	191
Chapter 36	201
Chapter 37	207
Chapter 38	213
Chapter 39	219
Chapter 40	225
Chapter 41	231
Chapter 42	237
Chapter 43	243
Epilogue	249
Author's Note	251
Other Books by this Author	253
Acknowledgments	255

All copyrights reserved under international copyright law KAREN BRADY THE PUBLISHER.

No part of this publication may be reproduced, transmitted, downloaded, decompiled, stored on any information storage and retrieval system, reverse-engineered or distributed in any form by any means, including photocopying, recording, or other electronic or mechanical methods, now known or in the future without the prior written permission of the publisher, Karen Brady, except in the case of brief quotations embodied in critical reviews and certain other non-commercial uses permitted by copyright law.

This eBook has been provided for your personal use only. Any permission requests please write to the publisher, addressed, "Attention: Permissions Coordinator" at the email address below
karenbradyauthor@gmail.com

Disclaimer

This is a work of fiction. All the characters, places, organisations, and events portrayed in this novel are used fictitiously. Any resemblance to actual events, or persons, living or dead, is entirely coincidental.

To my mother whose voice still guides me

To my hairdresser in Dubai who inspired this story

To Gerard, Isabella, Blaise and my extended family

o my loved ones gone too soon and never forgotten

To my friends everywhere on earth

Especially to my readers

Dubai – Present Day

Grace Peters lay still, her hands trembling as she gripped onto her son, little Darcy. Gently holding her hand over his mouth in the darkness of the hidden void under the bed.

She swallowed the bile to the back of her throat and held her breath. She couldn't hear Captain Lincoln but the smell of his cigar smoke reassured her that he was near.

Her legs were numb, curled with her knees bent in the small space as her son lay still between them, but that was the least of her troubles.

* * *

A loud helicopter hovered over the sailboat. The team of coastguards' boots thumped as they boarded the deck from their military vessel.

"Where is the boy?" a uniformed Emirate guard asked in broken English.

Captain Lincoln stared at him. Wiping his grey hair from his wrinkled sun-drenched face with his cigar in his fingers.

"What boy?" he asked in his calm Californian accent.

He'd successfully smuggled many innocents out of Dubai.

Chapter One

Grace Peters sat at her desk at the London law firm. Signing corporate documents ready for the impatient courier to deliver to her new client. As irritating as he was, he provided the distraction she needed to keep her mind off the following day's visit to her wife's family home in Dubai.

Her wife, Nadia Aktoum, hadn't had any contact with her parents for seven years, since she and Grace had both graduated at Oxford. Her parents had planned for her to marry her cousin. A customary arrangement since they were children.

Nadia had initially accepted her intended fate to appease her parents and adhere to family tradition, but once she had arrived at Oxford and met Grace, she refused.

Nadia's mother Fatima remained bitter and outraged, until recently when her health deteriorated and she invited them over together to settle family differences and meet Nadia and Grace's son Darcy.

Grace sympathised knowing that her wife would never be truly happy until her maternal mother accepted her for who she was. Just as her own caring family had.

Grace pushed the bundle of documents into a large brown envelope and shoved them into the courier's hand.

The tube train was packed in rush hour. She stood tall in her smart black professional suit and held onto the overhead bar. Her black leather briefcase in one hand and her matching shoulder bag slung over her right shoulder as it tugged at her long blonde flawless hair.

As he entered her compartment, a man tripped and almost pushed her over, without an apology.

I won't miss tube journeys, when I'm holidaying in Dubai.

The train halted at Hackney Station. Outside in the cold she picked up her pace, rain drizzled on her without an umbrella. She smiled to herself, looking forward to being home and helping Nadia pack for their trip.

She turned into their pathway and saw Nadia already in the bedroom upstairs. Nadia was too excited to wait and had already started packing without waiting for her.

Hidden Evil

The weight of the preparation for the last day before a holiday lifted as she opened their newly renovated yellow Victorian door, slipped off her shiny black heels, bag and jacket, and placed her briefcase down in the hallway.

She walked into the kitchen and poured them both a glass of red wine. Inhaling the aroma of their delicious dinner cooking in the oven, Grace made her way upstairs.

"You're early!" Nadia smiled as she took the wine and sipped it after Grace kissed her.

Grace reciprocated the kiss and smile. "I'm on time." She sipped her wine.

"How was your last day at the office?" Grace asked.

"I managed to finalise the Devlins' divorce, without further insults from Mr Devlin. That's a bonus for me." They high-fived.

"How was *your* last day?" Nadia enquired.

"Better now it's over. I can concentrate on you two for two whole weeks." Grace smiled again, not wanting to bore herself or Nadia with her corporate clients' demands after hours.

"Darcy is getting dropped home soon from his violin lesson. Jonesy kindly offered as he knows we're busy packing. I bet he'll be relieved to get a break from the violin for a couple of weeks." Nadia laughed while tying her long black hair up into a scraggy ponytail.

"Mom insisted she got him lessons whilst he's young, to appreciate musical instruments." Grace mimicked her mother's voice, the broad Birmingham pronunciation of 'mom' rather than the standard 'mum' used in other areas of England. "You know it isn't my idea to burden the poor boy so early." Grace sipped her wine.

* * *

When the packing was done, they moved downstairs to finish off cooking dinner. Darcy arrived home looking worn out after a long day at school and the music lesson. He was just in time to sit and eat their last dinner together for two weeks before his bedtime.

"What's the first thing you're going to say to Grandma Fatima?" Nadia asked Darcy while serving him chocolate ice cream.

"I don't know," Darcy replied with a yawn.

"We've gone over this a few times, sweetheart. When you meet her, say 'marhabaan alijida'. It means 'hello Grandma' in Arabic. She'll fall instantly in love with you." Nadia smiled at the idea of the introduction she had been wishing for to finally come true.

"I'm very excited to meet her and Grandpa."

They both put Darcy to bed exhausted without his usual bedtime story, before they cleaned up the kitchen and retired early to bed themselves ready for their early morning flight from Heathrow to Dubai International Airport.

Chapter Two

They boarded the flight with ease. Sitting together in a row of three, each with their own television screens in the back of the seats in front. During take-off they held hands and closed their eyes whilst giggling with excitement.

Darcy watched cartoons as the food was served and his parents ate theirs without wine. Nadia didn't want to arrive stinking of alcohol. Her parents were Muslim and wouldn't approve.

"Let's go over things again, things we can and can't say or do when we arrive," Nadia suggested.

"Not again. Stop fretting. I know the drill." Grace knew Nadia was nervous and why they'd gone over the rules, countless times.

"Just once more please! My parents will accept you into their home, but there are a few things that we must respect in their home. I know it's difficult for you but I really need this and it's only two weeks. Afterwards, we can get back to our normal lives, with me happy that Darcy has met his estranged grandparents.

"Firstly, we'll have to sleep in separate rooms. I'll take Darcy in with me because I gave birth to him and my mother will expect that. Secondly, we can't drink any alcohol. Thirdly, absolutely no touching or kissing. It's forbidden in public for anyone to kiss on the lips anyway, but we can't even kiss on the cheek in front of my family. It's got to be perfect for them and I know you understand that. Finally, no mention of you not going to church anymore. I've told them you're practising still so that's enough for them to digest."

"I know, I know. I promise to be on my best behaviour. I'm happy they no longer wish to disown you. I remember when I first met your mother, how she loved the idea that your best friend was the daughter of a British diplomat. We got on so well back then. I can't forget the sadness in her eyes when she discovered we were lovers."

"My parents aren't just religious they're extremely conservative. They're also parents who see their children as a reflection of themselves. I've already told you how Mother is more extreme than my father, she has an antiquated way of believing how I should live my life and has found it impossible until now, it seems, to accept the one I have chosen to marry. I know it's difficult for you to understand how they've ignored me for years, but all I want is for them to accept Darcy and you. It's really important to me and I'm prepared to bite my lip for their blessing and our happiness."

Hidden Evil

* * *

They both settled into a movie. Grace was keen to arrive and get the greetings over with, so she could enjoy Nadia's contentment upon her reunion with her family.

At Dubai International hundreds of passengers lined up for security checks. Grace had booked the tickets and spent extra on express checkout. She knew Darcy would be tired after a seven-hour flight and he would be too excited to nap on the plane.

Swiftly through customs they were greeted by the family driver, Ahmed, who was waiting for them as they exited customs, holding up a sign for Nadia Aktoum.

After pleasant introductions upon first meeting Nadia, he led them swiftly outside into a waft of thirty-six-degree heat and high humidity. It was late afternoon and too hot to be outside anywhere. They followed Ahmed to a white Hummer SUV, an unapologetically boxy and impossibly wide vehicle.

He placed their bags into the boot and gave them all a bottle of chilled water from the small cooler, after they had clicked their seatbelts inside the spacious and luxurious military vehicle. Darcy was still sweating, even after he'd removed his hoodie. The cool air-conditioning was an instant relief.

Ahmed manoeuvred the car out of the airport traffic to reach the highway. He'd been the family driver for just over five years. Selected and recruited by Nadia's father Mohammed, who'd preferred a local

Emirati driver, paying handsomely for his services to the family, over other nationalities that most families employed, thus avoiding costly salaries of experienced high-salaried locals.

"Wow! The architecture, it's so diverse. The tall shiny new buildings look very glamorous and glitzy," Grace remarked.

"A lot's changed since I was here. There are definitely more buildings along the Sheikh Zayed Road than before. They've filled the gaps in between the old buildings to build new taller ones. My parents have moved to Emirates' Hills. That wasn't built when I lived here. We used to live in Al Barsha in a villa near to here." She pointed as they drove past.

Ahmed turned into the road towards Emirates' Hills. "That was where I first became your family's driver. So much has changed around here and throughout the whole of Dubai. The development is nonstop. Whole new neighbourhoods have been built with new shopping malls and hotels everywhere. It's unrecognisable now."

He was met at the security barriers where a guard greeted him with acknowledgement and checked on the passengers before lifting the barrier to allow them to enter the private luxury complex.

Trees of palms lined along the pavements facing gated private mansions. Each had their own contemporary or Arabesque design. Ahmed stopped and waited for their large gold-sprayed iron decorative gates to slowly open.

Hidden Evil

* * *

Nadia squeezed Grace's hand in anticipation. As the car pulled up outside their cream mansion, she held her breath at the sight of its magnitude and spectacular architectural beauty.

Her parents were standing outside the front doorway to greet them. The butterflies in her stomach fluttered. She was so overwhelmed, tears welled up in her dark eyes and poured down her olive cheeks.

* * *

Grace turned round to embrace her but stopped herself and instead squeezed her hand in recognition.

Nadia jumped out of the car and ran to her parents. After a long embrace she introduced Grace first and then Darcy, they invited them inside. Grace felt strangely uneasy. She hadn't expected any embrace herself but felt sickened that Darcy, the Aktoums' grandson, didn't receive one.

Ahmed was left outside to carry their suitcases and organise them with the maids into their respective rooms.

"Dinner is almost ready, come into the day room for pre-dinner drinks," Fatima Aktoum suggested.

A maid arrived immediately with a tray full of soft drinks. Nadia sat contented between her parents on a large floral sofa. Grace held Darcy's hand on another matching sofa facing theirs.

"What do you want to say to Grandma, Darcy?"

Grace asked, feeling his dismay at the unique situation he had been placed in.

"Marhabaan alijida," he shyly whispered holding his head down.

They all laughed as Grandpa Mohammad reached out to shake his tiny hand.

Fatima still hadn't hugged her grandson.

Nadia seemed too overwhelmed to notice but Grace was feeling more uneasy than she had done when they'd arrived.

Chapter Three

Jamila, the younger sister, a spitting image of Nadia, arrived soon after, looking glamorous in her blue lace designer dress with her handsome husband and two smartly dressed daughters. Two brothers arrive with their wives and children. The expansive dining area was ready to serve their family feast.

"Darcy and I need to get washed up for dinner. I feel like I've been wearing my jeans all week," Grace said.

"Of course, let me show you to your rooms." Jamila smiled then walked ahead of them.

They followed her through a long hallway with walls covered in beautiful family portraits. Nadia admired them but looked around, as there didn't seem to be one of herself.

"You're not there," Jamila whispered then put her bottom lip above her top lip, showing a sad face.

Nadia looked surprised but Grace could see that she was noticeably upset.

Grace took Darcy by the hand and led him up the large open Italian-marbled French-styled stairs with iron cast decorative railings and into her bedroom to avoid him seeing Nadia upset.

Grace could see that Darcy was already overwhelmed by the crowd of noisy strangers. Nadia followed them along the landing as she instinctively held back her tears of disappointment.

"Enjoy your shower, sweetheart. I'll see you in ten minutes." Nadia knelt down, kissed and hugged him, before he took off to shower. He smiled in her warm embrace.

Inside her bedroom Grace noticed that her clothes had been unpacked and neatly put away by a maid. It seemed far too big to sleep in alone with floor-to-ceiling mirrors and a walk-in wardrobe layered with drawers and rails each side.

After further introductions at the dinner table, the conversation flowed. The maids served the delicious meal of Arabic delights. Everyone wanted to hear about Nadia's life in London and her stressful career as a family lawyer. They asked questions about Darcy, his school, and what he liked to do in his spare time.

No one asked anything about Grace; where she had come from, what she did for a living or how she lived her life in London, as if she almost didn't exist.

She began to feel more and more uneasy and missed her usual glass of red wine with dinner.

The evening was long and the travellers were exhausted. They retired to their respective rooms after saying goodnight to everyone. Grace kissed and hugged

Darcy as she put him to bed in Nadia's room. Mother Fatima stayed in there until Grace left, so she and Nadia had no chance of a goodnight embrace.

Grace felt perturbed by Fatima's presence but remained on her best behaviour as promised and went quietly to bed.

Chapter Four

Nadia was crying as she spoke in her mother tongue to her parents. "I love her. Why can't you accept that I'm happy and in love?"

"We can never accept that you are living a life against Allah," Fatima said. "It's not in our religion to accept it. It's illegal here as you are fully aware, it holds a prison sentence, sometimes a death sentence. If anyone outside of this family knew, we would all be ostracised from our community and you would be in prison!"

"I know all that, Mother, I just didn't realise you still felt this way. I came here by your invitation, to introduce our son to you and receive your blessing. I love you and desperately want your approval. I thought you'd changed to respect my happiness. I thought your cancer scare had warmed you towards acceptance."

* * *

Grace unexpectedly slept in. She was awakened by the sound of voices in the day room. The voices were initially quiet and then became much louder.

Grace couldn't understand the whole conversation as her Arabic wasn't fluent, but she knew instinctively that it wasn't the warm greeting Nadia had received the previous day.

Grace quickly showered and went downstairs to join them and offer a distraction.

She smiled as she entered after seeing Darcy's head down in despair at his mother's sadness. "Are we ready for the waterpark, Darcy?"

Nadia had been teaching Grace and Darcy Arabic, so Grace knew that he had understood more of the argument than she had as Darcy found it easier to learn the language than she had.

"I'm ready." He looked up with wide eyes that told her to get him out of the room.

"Come on," Nadia blurted, waving her arms in frustration.

Ahmed the family driver was summoned to take the three of them to the Atlantis Hotel waterpark for the day.

Grace was concerned about the argument and keen to know in full detail what they had been arguing about, but wouldn't ask in front of Ahmed, and didn't want to subject Darcy to, or involve him in, their adult conversation.

Once they had purchased entrance tickets, they sat at the children's poolside and saw Darcy instantly perk up playing on the slides with the other kids.

Hidden Evil

"What was all that about earlier?" Grace enquired as she settled onto her comfortable beach bed mattress, relieved to be outside and away from the tension boiling in the mansion.

"My mother's still in denial about how I'm living my life, but I'm here to change that. It's not going to be as easy as I'd thought. When she invited us over, I wrongly presumed that acknowledgement was acceptance. She's always been stubborn, but I'm surprised she remains so. I know it's because of her religious beliefs and the laws here that's holding her back. She's refused to give me her blessing still, but I'm not giving up so easily.

"She wants me to accompany her to the mosque for Friday prayers tomorrow. I have agreed to go and look forward to it, but mainly I'm going to show her I still have my faith and live by it always. I'm determined to do all I can to sway her into acceptance of the way I live my life which hasn't meant leaving my faith behind."

"Let's go on the slides and have some fun. Come on, I want you to enjoy your time in your stunning city. Try to take your mind off it for a while I'm sure she'll come around to acceptance once she gets to know more about Darcy and how truly happy we all are."

Nadia forced a smile walking toward the slides to play with Darcy but the knot in her belly would not disappear.

I hope this trip is going to be worth it!

When Ahmed the driver dropped them back to Emirates' Hills, dinner was ready. The three of them ate almost in silence with Nadia's parents who agreed to look after Darcy that evening, in an attempt to bond with him.

"We are looking forward to learning who our grandson is," Fatima said with a warm smile touching his cheek as he smiled shyly at her.

"Are you sure you'll be able to manage, Mother?" Nadia was elated at the idea of them bonding.

"I'm rested now, the doctors have reassured me that the cancer is in remission. I have enough help here in my home and I intend to live my life to its fullest, just as Allah wishes."

Father Mohammad smiled along with her.

After dinner, Grace and Nadia quickly changed to go clubbing. Ahmed dropped them off at Five Hotel on Palm Jumeirah at 23.00.

"What time shall I collect you?" he asked Nadia.

"I'm not sure where we'll be later after we've partied the night away and explored the new Palm Jumeriah bars and clubs. I'll call a taxi home later. Thanks for the ride here. Good night." Nadia knew she needed to ditch him to enjoy the exclusive private party scene.

They drank sugary non-alcoholic cocktails, watching everyone else consume copious amounts of alcohol at the bar, until midnight.

Hidden Evil

"I checked online for an underground Thursday night club before we got on the plane," Nadia told Grace. "I really want to show you how we enjoy Dubai, with its restrictions, to the fullest. Come on, drink up. Taxis are lining up outside. We can jump in one of those instead of using our app. We're going to Frond 14 to party with the gals." Nadia laughed, stood and slugged down her last drop of lemonade cocktail.

* * *

They arrived at the long driveway to the private mansion on Palm Jumeirah which looked empty from the outside. The lady on the door only opened once the taxi drove away. She asked to see their ID.

"I see you're a member of the Aktoum family." She looked worried.

"Yes I am. My father is the military general. He doesn't know I'm here and I want it to remain that way. Please don't have any concerns. I'm here for no other reason than to enjoy your hospitality. I'm not a radical fundamentalist ready to oust you to the police. I just want to show my wife how we party underground in Dubai." Nadia placed her arm around Grace and pulled her in close.

Grace smiled at the lady, offering reassurance.

The lady smiled back at the happy couple. Once convinced, she led them into a large room full of dancing women from all nationalities of various ages.

Loud music thumped from the overhead speakers above the DJ. Women sat on white sixties-style chairs that hung from the ceiling, sipping cocktails and champagne. The cigarette smoke swirled around the room. High-backed purple velvet sofas adorned the outer rim of the dance floor, where a disco globe spun above, showing all the colours of the rainbow.

A young waitress dressed in black appeared and asked them if they would like to be seated. They followed her, walking past the trendy white bar and sat at the edge of the dance floor.

"Do you have cocktails without alcohol?" Nadia asked.

"Yes, but we don't usually serve them in here." She laughed, gripping hold of her tray.

"We're on our best behaviour staying with my parents and tomorrow I'm respectfully attending Friday prayers. Can we have cocktails with zero alcohol please?"

The waitress moved towards the bar to place the order. Grace took Nadia by the hand and led them straight onto the dance floor.

"It's weird dancing in a club without a proper drink."

They echoed laughter as they enjoyed the rhythm and beats helping them to let their hair down and relax before the next round of struggles back at the family mansion.

* * *

Hidden Evil

Five hours later, both exhausted from dancing the night away, they sat to finish off their last cocktail of the night.

"I'm beat, shall we go?" Nadia asked.

"Me too, let's."

"So, how did you like your club experience?" Nadia asked, as they walked outside into the hot humidity just before sunrise whilst she ordered a taxi from her phone app and sat on an outside chair waiting.

"It's hardly London, but I've had a lovely night in a cool underground venue with friendly people. A bit like what it might have been back in London in the sixties, with clandestine clubbing. It's the first time I've gone clubbing without drinking, but at least we won't have a hangover tomorrow." She smiled holding her long hair up in her hands to wipe the sweat off the back of her neck.

Morning call for Fajr prayer echoed everywhere from the surrounding mosques and the taxi's radio that dropped them back to Emirates' Hills.

"That's the first time I've heard the call for prayer, it seems eerie to me, like we're in the twilight zone or somewhere alien." Grace laughed.

"The call for prayer comes five times a day in mostly built-up areas but not everywhere. We can't hear it where we live or on the Palm, because there aren't any mosques there. I don't think it's eerie, I'm used to it. I remember hearing church bells when I first arrived in Oxford. Now that was weird, but I eventually got used to it and enjoyed the sound."

* * *

Once inside the mansion they gulped down chilled water from a fridge in the hallway. Upstairs Grace went into Nadia's room to kiss her and Darcy goodnight. She noticed the black attire laid on Nadia's bed.

"How long has it been since you wore a full abaya?" Grace whispered as she touched the garment laid out ready for the following day's Friday prayers at the mosque.

"Around seven years, since the last time I came home in the summer holidays from Oxford. I only ever wore it on Fridays to prayers with my mother and sister. I like the mystique of wearing it. It makes me feel invisible but also secure, and it expresses my values towards my faith and culture. My parents never made it compulsory for us to wear daily. It's not so strict in Dubai for Emiratis to wear it, unless you work in government or banks, where you're greeting and meeting men. We're liberated women in my family, you know!" She rolled her eyes at the daunting task ahead, towards the ultimate liberation of her mother to accept her as she was.

Chapter Five

Grace slept in longer than anticipated and missed Nadia at breakfast. She showered and went to find Darcy. She searched throughout the house, calling his name, but couldn't find him anywhere.

"Have you seen Darcy?" Grace asked a maid in the kitchen.

"He left early with Jamila and her daughters to go shopping in the mall. Would you like breakfast?"

"Er, yes please, I'll make myself eggs. Hasn't Jamila gone with Nadia and Fatima to Friday prayers as arranged?"

"You sit, madam. How do you like your eggs?" the maid insisted as she pulled out a chair at the kitchen table.

"Scrambled please." Grace smiled, feeling uncomfortable that she was a guest in a wealthy household full of maids that did everything for you.

Another maid appeared and the colleagues chatted quietly in Amharic. Grace felt she was eavesdropping, so took her phone out of her jeans pocket to check for any messages from Nadia. Nothing.

The deliciously soft salty eggs melted on Grace's tongue as she sipped her warm fresh coffee.

"May I use the pool?" she asked the maid as she took her plate and cup to the sink.

"Yes madam, towels and water are outside ready for you."

"Thanks ladies, the eggs were perfect." Grace smiled and walked out the kitchen to the large hallway and heard a loud banging that felt like it almost knocked the front door down.

A maid hurried and opened the door.

Grace froze.

Two policemen marched in and handcuffed her.

"Miss Peters...You are under arrest for the murder of Nadia Aktoum!" the older of the two policemen told her.

"WHAT?" Grace shrieked, but allowed herself to be cuffed.

They bundled her into a police car parked directly outside the large front door.

"Where are you taking me? Where's Nadia?"

"BE QUIET!" was the only answer she received.

"I'm a lawyer. I know my rights. You can't just arrest me without reading me my rights."

The policemen said nothing.

Chapter Six

Grace arrived at Al Barsha police station. A wide, almost empty, building with scattered staff and lots of dark brown office doors. It was an old building but had been renovated into a contemporary setting by an internal architect with little idea of how to design modern interiors.

A uniformed policewoman, dressed in light and dark shades of green with matching hijab under her smartly set pillbox hat, marched her swiftly downstairs in silence and placed her in a small cell that adorned only a sink, toilet and bed. The policewoman uncuffed Grace.

"I want to see Nadia," Grace pleaded.

"That's the woman who has been reported missing this morning by General Aktoum, who suspects that you murdered her and disposed of her body last night. The general himself has brought these charges on you. We will be ready to interview you in due course," the policewoman replied sternly and left the cell.

Grace was speechless as she sat on the filthy stinking bed in shock, wondering where Nadia could be and if this was really happening. The reality finally sunk in when the policewoman clunked the cell door shut and left her alone inside with the horror of imprisonment.

Grace felt her phone vibrate in her pocket. She hadn't been searched yet. She quickly dialled Nadia's number, which went directly to voicemail. Grace rose to her feet in panic as she called her father in London with trembling hands.

"Hi Gracie, how's Dubai?" he asked pleasantly.

"Not good, Dad. I've been arrested, I'm in a prison cell near the Mall of the Emirates."

"What the hell?"

"Mohammed's had me arrested by reporting Nadia missing earlier this morning. He's accusing me of murder and disposing of her body last night. It's pathetic. I can't fathom what he's up to, but you know how much power he has here."

"My god. I *do* know how corrupt those top officials over there are but I can't believe he'd go this far. Where do you think she is? Why do you think he's got you out the way with these ridiculous accusations?"

"As far as I know, she went with her mother to Friday prayers. I can't understand what's going on or why he's had me arrested. I've tried calling her but it's going to voicemail. I don't know what to do. I've heard the horror stories of being locked up here without any rights, guilty until proven innocent."

"Don't panic. I have a friend with legal contacts

there, I'll get in touch with him now and get him on the case as soon as possible. Don't say anything without a lawyer, you know that, love."

"Of course. Dad, please hurry. It's vile in here. I need to get out. I'm worried for Nadia, and I have no idea where Darcy is. He went shopping with Jamila this morning before I woke up, but she was supposed to go to Friday prayers with Nadia and Fatima."

"Keep your phone close. I'll call you straight back."

"Okay. Thanks, Dad. Bye."

Grace went over in her mind the events of the previous night. They'd arrived home and gone to bed with water after kissing sleeping Darcy. She felt an overwhelming surge of guilt for not waking before they had left that morning.

*Why hadn't they woken me to say goodbye? Where **are** they? What's going on?*

She had more questions than answers as her phone in her pocket vibrated.

"Hi Dad." She swallowed hard and felt a lump in her throat as she held back her frustrated tears.

"I've found a lawyer. Rita. She's on her way to the station, and will be there in around thirty minutes. She's an expert on the laws over there, with a lot of experience working with a defence firm for foreigners, mainly Westerners."

"Thanks Dad. I don't understand what's

happening. I've been denied legal due process and they didn't bother to search me."

"We both know how Dubai leaders are promoting their country to outsiders as a playground for fun and investment, whilst withholding the fact that their laws are completely different to ours. Be very careful what you say. A lot of people are falsely imprisoned, only for the authorities to find something else to detain them for. There's a lot of high-level corruption and illegal torture over there."

"I know. I just didn't think I'd be the one in a cell. I'm okay, don't worry as they have nothing on me, extraordinary claims need extraordinary evidence which they have none."

"I love you, Gracie. Remain vigilant as my diplomatic immunity doesn't cover you as an adult, but I've informed Rita and she's calling in all my favours. Make sure you ring me as soon as you've got more information."

Grace put the phone on silent and hid it back in her jeans pocket. She paced the cell floor. Whispering voices of women could be heard in the adjoining cells, from the female-only section of the hold.

The same policewoman arrived and opened the cell, handcuffed Grace, and led her down vast corridors of white painted walls then upstairs to an interview room.

Chapter Seven

"Hello, I'm Rita. Robert Peters sent me," the lady said in her high-pitched Sydney accent, holding her right hand out to shake Grace's. Rita was dressed in a professional black trouser suit, white neck-bowed blouse and matching black flat slip-on easy leather shoes.

"Nice to meet you. It's a relief. Thanks for getting here so fast. I'm impressed."

"Leave us to talk." Rita summoned the policewoman to close the door behind her as Rita placed her briefcase on the empty table and took out a notepad and pen.

"Pleasure to meet you too, Grace. First a few things you need to know before we go any further. I must stress that you never speak without being spoken to and offer only yes or no answers as much as you can, okay. Nadia is the daughter of the head of military, a powerful man with a corrupt reputation who can create any situation he desires to keep you locked up."

"I'm aware he's in a very powerful position, but I didn't know about any *obvious* corruption. What sort of corruption is he involved in?"

"Too much to tell you in detail but he's the head of Secret Services, above the level of government and the sheikh of Dubai. He's top tier of the hidden hierarchy here and the most powerful of them."

"I had no idea and I don't think Nadia knows either, but he's got me falsely arrested so I understand his power. He knows Nadia is my wife and I love her. We married under civil partnership in England. He knows I wouldn't harm her or anyone. And I'm a lawyer."

"Ah, that's your first mistake. You absolutely must not give the authorities any other reason to hold you than the initial one of your wife's disappearance and the accusation of murder. You're lucky he's protecting himself by not arresting you for illicit sexual activity, but he needs the other party for that to stick and he won't put his own flesh and blood on the line.

"They'd throw the key away for months until trial and then give you a hefty fine with a long sentence for illegally carrying out sexual acts in this country. It's a strictly forbidden criminal offence. Sharia Law carries a death sentence for severe crimes. It isn't quite Nazism, Hitler isn't killing minorities anymore, nobody has been put to death for this type of illegal misconduct here in years, but most people of different orientation, if caught, remain incarcerated, often without trial. You must have known that before you arrived?" Rita screwed up her green oval eyes awaiting an answer.

"Yes, I'm aware of Sharia Law. It was a risk to visit I know but I came here to support Nadia, and I thought we'd be safe in her parents' home. Nadia wants so much to receive acceptance and blessings from her estranged mother."

"So, what's happened to Nadia, where do you think she is?" Rita asked.

"All I know is that she was supposed to go to Friday prayers with her mother and sister this morning."

"The police aren't saying that and they have security footage to back up their allegation. Are you ready to see it?" Rita said with urgency in her voice.

"Yes."

"Wait for my nod before replying yes or no to their questions. I'll call them in so we can get this over with."

She left the room as Grace bit her nails, her throat dry and thirsty.

A few minutes later, which seemed longer, a green-uniformed policeman bounced into the room with Rita. He sat opposite them at the small table and opened a laptop ready to show them CCTV security footage. He placed Nadia's mobile phone onto the table next to the laptop.

No preparation to record the interview under protocol was taken which Grace considered highly suspicious but she waited to see the evidence.

She wanted to ask how they had Nadia's mobile

phone but resisted the temptation, adhering to Rita's instructions.

The video showed Grace and Nadia the previous night leaving in a taxi from the large villa on Frond 14 Palm Jumeirah.

He pointed to the video. "Note the time you left here. 01.05."

The time on the video isn't right. We left the club just before sunset. We were on the dance floor at 01.05. What's going on?

The second security video shows Grace arriving at 05.50 alone at Emirates Hills. The situation was becoming unbearable for Grace. She wanted to scream 'LIARS'.

"What happened to Nadia during those hours from 01.05 to 05.50?" the policeman asked.

Grace looked at Rita for the nod to speak then she held her head in her hands and breathed heavily before calmly looking up and answering.

"We left the Palm around 05.35. The time must be wrong on the security camera and we both arrived together shortly after at Emirates' Hills. How come Nadia isn't showing on the video footage?"

"She's not showing on the footage because you arrived back alone. That's why you're here, so we can ask you if you know of her whereabouts."

Grace could hardly breathe or believe what she was hearing. It was a ridiculous accusation but the tension remained as Rita's earlier words reminded her of the corruption Nadia's father was doing at the very top of it all.

Hidden Evil

"Can we obtain a copy of the video footage?" Rita asked, showing no emotion.

"Yes, I will get you a copy." The policeman left the room.

"This is bullshit. It looks like someone has tampered with the security footage both ends. Can you ask him how he got Nadia's phone? She booked the taxi from her app last night. It will show the correct time and the lady on the door waved us goodbye. We heard the morning prayer loud and clear around 05.40. Can they get the taxi driver who dropped us both off to come and give a statement?" Grace stood and banged her fist on the table.

"That's a serious accusation, you can't accuse the head of military of tampering with his own security cameras. That'll be added as an offence. You need to calm down so we can figure this out. I will ask to inspect the phone. Please sit down and try to be quiet."

Grace sat down and put her head in her hands again in total disbelief.

The policeman reappeared with a flash drive and handed it to Rita before she asked him, "How do you have Nadia's phone? Can we study it?"

"Her father gave it to me. He told me he found it on the Palm on Frond 14 in a ladies' club this morning. It needs charging."

Grace had a dozen questions running through her mind but remained quietly composed in his presence. Rita was a Dubai law expert, Grace continued to remind herself.

He left the room to charge the phone, closing the door behind him.

"How do they know we went to the club?" Grace asked. "We ditched the family driver at the hotel entrance and stayed for an hour before jumping in a local taxi to the villa. Her father must have had someone follow us last night. But why?" Grace bawled as she waved her arms in the air.

"Her father has access to cell tower information. He can see where she was last night without following her. He doesn't need anyone's permission to get information on his daughter. He has collaborators everywhere working for him and doing whatever he wants. Nadia is an unmarried woman in the eyes of the law and therefore belongs to her father until she marries. Under law he has total control over her."

"Fucking misogynists," Grace snapped.

"Welcome to the real Dubai." Rita folded her arms, walked around the table and sat on the edge pushing back her dark bobbed hair away from her face.

A policewoman brought bottles of water into the room and left them on the table without speaking.

"Can you get me out of here today? I want to be with Darcy. He must be scared without us."

"Not until Sunday I'm afraid. I'll request a hearing in front of a judge first thing to get you out on bail. I'll offer your passport as security. Let's hope Nadia shows up by then. I'll do some of my own investigating and collect your things from Emirates' Hills, and bring you a suit for court. Those jeans won't be allowed."

"Thank you. I don't have a smart suit with me. I

didn't think I'd need one on holiday. Will you please check on Darcy for me. I can't stand the idea of him being with *them*. I don't trust them. It seems they want me out of the way."

"Of course, I'll bring a suit early on Sunday for you. Afterwards, I can give you both a room in a safehouse on the Jumeirah Beach Road. We have other innocent victims awaiting trial staying there. Here's my card. Call me tomorrow around 6pm. I should have more information for you by then. Don't let them know you have your phone with you, they'll confiscate it. You're lucky its only scattered Friday staff today and they didn't search you yet."

The policeman returned with Nadia's phone and gave it to Rita. She passed it to Grace to open it using the passcode.

Grace checked the phone and saw all the apps had been removed as had the sim card, then showed it to Rita who asked, "Why has the sim been removed?"

"Mr Aktoum gave it me that way," the policeman replied.

"Can I take the phone to get some information from it?" Rita asked.

"Yes, we don't need it, we have the security footage for court on Sunday," he said then left the room.

"I'll put a sim card in it and reload the taxi app," Rita told Grace. "Can you write down Nadia's phone passcode and her password for emails? There might be a receipt via email, confirming the time of the taxi and the driver's name to find him for an interview."

"Thanks for your support. Has my father already paid your retaining fee?"

"Yes, and we'll be using his good name and his status in court to get bail if not a complete dismissal. I know it's easy for me to say but try not to worry about Darcy or Nadia. I'm sure her family won't harm them. It seems it's you they're after!"

Grace forced a smile feeling sick in her gut as she shook Rita's hand goodbye. She held out her hands to the policewoman ready to be cuffed for her return down to the cells.

The door slammed behind her again and she noticed the cracked badly plastered white paint on the walls fall off. The small space was airless and claustrophobic. Anxiety was no longer inanimate, it clawed at her from the inside out, straining to escape her body.

I wish we hadn't come here. We could be home drinking red wine and watching an old movie, sat on the sofa, all three of us together, happy as always.

Devotion to the truth is the hallmark of morality, there is no greater, nobler, more heroic form of devotion than the act of truth, as my professor at Oxford told me.

I need to control my thoughts of dread. If I can't control what I'm thinking then I can't control what I do or keep myself safe.

I need to stop being nervous.

I need to get out of here.

Chapter Eight

Early Saturday morning Rita's assistant Markus called the security at Emirates' Hills to request a visit to the Aktoum family mansion in order to collect Grace's belongings.

The security guard placed him on hold whilst he made a call to Fatima who agreed they could clear security and visit.

Rita stopped at the security gates and after showing her identification was swiftly allowed to pass.

After patiently waiting for the mansion entrance gates to open, she drove through and parked at the door expecting to meet Fatima Aktoum to gather further evidence.

A maid answered and offered a suitcase with Grace's belongings. Fatima was nowhere to be seen.

"May I speak to Madam Aktoum?" Rita asked politely.

"She's not available to come to the door but gave

instructions for me to give Grace's lawyer this letter and her suitcase."

Rita opened the envelope and read the content as Markus packed the suitcase into her car.

Darcy will remain with his aunt until Nadia is found safe and well. Make no attempt to obtain access to him. This will be strictly forbidden. Nadia is the biological mother and as grandparents we have complete control over him, under Sharia Law.

Fatima

Rita knew this to be true. Frustrated she pushed the envelope into her bag and drove away.

* * *

At 6pm Grace called Rita for an update.

"Hi Grace."

"Hello, do you have news on Nadia and Darcy?"

Rita read out the letter signed by Fatima.

"What the hell's going on with this family. Why are they keeping up this façade about Nadia's disappearance! Why hasn't Nadia come to get me out?"

"They obviously have something to hide and I'm hoping it's not as bad as other situations I've heard of here."

"What do you mean?"

"They are a prominent family and Mohammad is a whole other level of corruption. It looks like they'll never accept a lesbian daughter who refuses to adhere to their religious belief and their law. It's not only forbidden but utterly shameful for families here. I've

Hidden Evil

seen men and women disappear forever, some have been either killed in the name of HONOUR and buried out in the desert or locked up indefinitely at homes in secure locations. I must stress again, Grace, that Mohammad is a very powerful man."

"I had nightmares about this last night when I finally got to sleep, but it's just a bad dream, this can't be happening! They adore Nadia. I think they'll try anything to bring her back to their way of thinking, but I don't believe they'd ever harm her, I can't comprehend that," Grace whispered, feeling confident but not really believing herself anymore.

"I hope you're right. At least Darcy is safe," Rita said in a comforting voice.

"I know the laws are different here but don't they prefer the child to be with their father than their grandparents? My brother was the donor and his name is on the birth certificate, won't that help?"

"It might help us get a court date but it'll take months, if not years, to appear. The law prefers the child to stay within its religious homeland, rather than allow them outside of the country. It won't be easy; I have clients waiting years to be heard in family courts and it's very expensive to appeal."

"I can't stand it in here, not knowing where my wife is or if she's safe. I'm happy that Darcy is with Jamila and not Fatima but I can't stop worrying. Please do all you can to get me out tomorrow. Ask my father for anything you need to help force a dismissal. Surely they can't keep me locked up without any real evidence of being involved in Nadia's so-called disappearance.

The video footage is all they have but how are you going to prove it's been tampered with and get anyone to admit it?"

"I have an IT guy checking its validity but we're not going to be popular suggesting that the head of military is corrupt, so I'll have to tread lightly in court."

"Are you worried about doing that?"

"I've done it before because it's easy to prove innocence over crime. I'm working on the taxi driver being our number one witness to prove you both went into the front door of Emirates' house together at 05.56. It's on the taxi receipt in Nadia's email."

"That's the best news I've heard since I was arrested. Thank you for your diligence."

"I'll be with you at 07.00 tomorrow, bye."

"Bye."

Grace called her father to update him.

"I'm worried about you, Gracie, not just Nadia and Darcy. I didn't want you to go there but I understood how important it was for Nadia to reconcile and be happy. I've managed to speak with an old colleague of mine who knows the judge that you'll be in front of in court tomorrow. He will help all he can to get you out of this mess."

Grace could hear Susan her mother in the background asking for the phone.

"Hi darling. I can't begin to imagine how horrific it is. We're at Heathrow waiting our flight to be with you early tomorrow at court. Be strong, darling, you've always been braver than you think. We love you."

"I love you too, Mom. Thanks so much for coming

over to support me, it's comforting to know you'll both be here. My phone battery is dying. Have a safe flight I'll see you both tomorrow in court." She hung up, noticing her hands trembling again.

A policewoman appeared soon after and shoved a metal plate under the door hatch with a sloppy mess of boiled white rice, smothered in a watery brown peppered sauce accompanied by a plastic spoon.

Grace ate for the first time since the previous day's breakfast in the mansion but struggled to swallow it. She was hungry but didn't feel any joy eating the slushed food. The next day would be the most uncertain day of her life and nothing could take her mind off Nadia and Darcy.

She held her phone up close to look at her latest screensaver, a picture of the three of them smiling on the Emirates plane. Her phone bleeped its last bleep before dying.

Eventually she settled on the stinking bed, realising that it was the longest night of her life.

Fury built up inside her like she had never felt before.

Then she imagined she felt little Darcy stroking her hair. It was a comforting moment through all the stress of the last two days.

She dozed off, mentally exhausted.

Chapter Nine

Grace woke, startled, with a policewoman at her side.
"Get up. It's time to shower."
"What time is it?" Grace asked in a sleepy voice, thinking she was still dreaming.
"06.00."
The woman led her without handcuffs to the showers and stood watching her bathe herself standing there alone. The soap stank of old carbolic but it was still a relief to soap up her body and wash off the stinking filthy mattress odour.

Another policewoman delivered her breakfast of dates and stale bread to the cell. Grace ate them and almost heaved them back up as they slid along her tongue.

Rita arrived with a new navy skirt suit and black feminine low-heeled shoes for Grace. A white blouse finished off the smart look, ready to appear in front of the judge.

"How's your weekend?" Rita mused, while Grace dressed.

"Like a stay in the Burj Al Arab." Grace laughed, feeling relief at the idea of getting out of the cell forever.

A policewoman escorted her to the police car in handcuffs and sat next to her in the back. The policemen sat in the front and drove her to the criminal court building on Rihadh Street.

Rita followed them with her assistant, Markus, and Grace's parents Robert and Susan who waved frantically so she would see them.

Grace entered through the back entrance of the building, escorted either side like a criminal by the policemen. Where the other convicts awaited their trial. The only thing they all had in common was a worried solemn face.

Rita and her parents entered from the glamourous front of the enormous white building displaying the gold decorations and lush carpets along with United Arab Emirates flag boldly swaying in the air-conditioned waft.

The huge coloured pictures of the hierarchy of both current and long past Sheikhs adorned every wall.

As Grace entered the courtroom, she saw her parents looking worried in the seats near the back. Rita and Markus sat at a table to the left of the room.

Grace was led to the dock to sit and wait for the judge to enter. The two prosecution men wearing traditional Arabic Kandura with headdresses arrived and sat to the right of the room.

Hidden Evil

A man wearing white Kandura stood and spoke loudly to the occupants of the room. "All rise for the honourable judge."

Everyone stood and waited for the judge to sit and introduce himself, also wearing full white Kandura with headdress and extra black strings around his waist to present his status within judiciary hierarchy.

"Good morning, I am Honourable Judge Mohammad Bin Hamdan. I will be hearing the case against Grace Peters." He spoke stoically as he pulled up his sleeves and gestured for the prosecution to speak.

The first prosecution male addressed the judge.

"Grace Peters from Britain is detained for her silence concerning the untimely disappearance of Nadia Aktoum who was last seen leaving a ladies dinner party on Frond 14 of Palm Jumeirah last Thursday 11th May at 01.30 hours. She has not been seen or heard of since. Security footage has been shown to the court."

The judge summoned the defence to offer counter explanation. Rita confidently stood, looking impeccably professional in her black trouser court suit to address the judge.

"Your honour, we have meticulously put together our defence and wish to call Mr Ahmad as our first witness to the stand."

"Mr Ahmad, are you a taxi driver for the Uber company?" Rita asked.

"Yes."

"I have the receipt from missing person Nadia

Aktoum's email account stating that you picked her up at 05.35 on the morning of the 11th May from a private villa on Frond 14 Palm Jumeirah and dropped her off with the defendant Grace Peters at the home of Nadia's parents in Emirates' Hills at 05.55. Is that correct sir," she asked him sternly, under precision eye contact.

"Yes."

"Copies of both email receipts from Nadia and Mr Ahmad's log have been given into evidence this morning to the prosecution team. Therefore, we want the security footage dismissed as evidence," Rita confidently told the judge.

"Objection!" the prosecution barrister shouted.

"Overruled. New evidence has been offered showing that Miss Nadia arrived home safely with the defendant and left the Palm villa much later than the security footage shows. Do you have any further witnesses?" the judge asked Rita.

'Yes, I would like to call Mr Moons, an experienced technical analyst to the stand."

'Mr Moons, are you an employee of Proctors Security Systems and may I ask what you found wrong with the security footage?" Rita asked with conviction.

"Yes I am. It seems that the time on the first security footage has been changed and bought backwards in time about four hours and the second footage from Miss Nadia's arrival has been modified to remove her from the footage," he said in a nervous soft voice without any hint of accusation.

"Are you suggesting that video footage can be modified to this extent?" the judge asked.

"Yes, your honour. It can if you have the skill and know how to manipulate it. It's new technology with added after-effect software amongst others. That's the one I found used to modify this video footage," he replied slowly, as if proud of his knowledge and with conviction.

"Calling both defence and prosecution to the bench for private discussion," the judge said in frustration.

After a brief whispered conversation, they all sat back in their respective chairs.

"This case is dismissed. The defendant is free to leave without further investigation. I am satisfied with the email discovery. Case closed," Judge Bin Hamdan finalised, pounding his gavel and rising to leave the court.

Judges had witnessed many cases involving corruption involving Mohammad Aktoum. Judge Bin Hamdan knew exactly what he had conspired and was sickened by it, but there was nothing he, nor anyone else, could do to stop his corruption before court appearances and wasting of the court's time.

Grace had tears in her eyes. Her parents stood and cheered, whilst Rita thanked the judge for his verdict. She understood how difficult the judiciary in Dubai was and admired the judge for his unwavering courage to implement justice whenever he was able to.

They moved outside into the sunshine humidity and each one embraced Grace who was ready to find her wife and fight for their son .

"Any news on Darcy or Nadia?" Grace asked Rita.

"Darcy is still with Jamila at her house."

"I'm glad Jamila is taking care of him. At least he has her children to distract him but he should be with me. I intend to fight for him." Grace balled her fists as they walked away from the courthouse.

Chapter Ten

They all arrived at the Jumeirah Beach Hotel where her parents had booked them into a suite of rooms to share. Susan ordered room service of pots of tea and club sandwiches as the five of them sat around the dining table to discuss all the available options.

"I have a plan to get Darcy out of Dubai safely on a boat," Rita explained, "but it's not the legal way of waiting years going via the courts. I have a team of people who work with me in secret and we've managed to smuggle many children across the channel to India. Would you be interested in going down this route, Grace?"

Susan gasped. "No way, I can't believe you're considering this when he's legally Grace's son."

"We're in a country that practices Sharia Law using law to get convictions in their favour," Robert told her.

"I'm not happy either. As a law-abiding citizen and an enforcer of law, I'm not ready to become a people smuggler but there isn't anything else legally we can do, Mom," Grace replied.

Rita nodded. "It's brave of you, Grace, to agree. It *is* the fastest way for results."

She addressed Susan. "We can begin a case for custody but this type of lawsuit will be very different from Grace's case this morning. Your husband's position as a diplomat has greatly influenced a speedy court appearance today with favourable results. Mohammed's corruption didn't go unnoticed by the judge and gave us justice but he's not on family court cases. He only deals in criminal negligence and high crime murders.

"Custody cases are put to the back of the line, especially if you're not an Emirati citizen; they go further down the pile and take years to appear into family court. Often with three or four separate appearances and appeals.

"The judicial system here is very slow, especially as the Aktoum grandparents have already showed how far towards corruption they're prepared to go to get what they want. It's a huge risk to go down the legal route and I can't offer you a favourable outcome," Rita explained.

Grace nodded. "I'll do it. If I'm caught smuggling my son out illegally, what is that sentence likely to be?"

"People smuggling carries a sentence of up to forty years, but we haven't been caught, because I have reliable teams with expertise willing to help us," Rita assured her.

Susan shook her head. "This is ridiculous, we're not

Hidden Evil

criminals. There must be another way around this. What if we bring over Jonathan to claim custody as he's on Darcy's birth certificate."

"That *would* be the legal way to go about it as Grace wouldn't be recognised as his legal guardian," Rita replied. "A civil marriage isn't only not recognised but considered a criminal offence and could carry life imprisonment, so we couldn't take that route."

"Maybe we could go and talk to Nadia's parents and beg them to let us have him back?" Susan suggested in tears.

"There's no point, Mom. Look what they've done so far to get me out of the way." Grace held out her hands to comfort her mother, feeling braver than ever, and hugged her.

Robert continued. "Britain doesn't have any extradition treaty with UAE because we are aware of their treatment of prisoners, which goes against human rights. Excessive torture and sometimes death occurs in the prison system here. Let's get you both out and back to safety in London. We'll all feel better once we get out of this country."

"Okay," Grace said, "let's do it. How long does it take to sail to India?"

"About seven days," Rita replied.

"That's doable and *must* be done. Darcy's with Jamila who's a kind woman, we've always got on well. She speaks regularly with us online and gives us updates on the family. I'll ask her if I can see Darcy once more before I leave, without telling her parents or giving the game away. The boat must be ready for us to sail within minutes, once he's in my grasp," Grace stated.

"I'll set it up immediately," Rita said. "We have a dedicated couple at the offshore sailing club, who've been helping us for years to get innocent people out of here, especially the ones who have given their passports into the police for bail security bond. It's not expensive, they only ask for a donation for their cause along with fuel and food cost of a round trip."

Robert butted in. "We'll fly home and get a new passport for Darcy and all our visas to enter India and fly straight out there to wait for you to arrive. Darcy needs a stamp upon entering at the port and can then travel securely with my diplomatic immunity from India by plane."

"Get a replacement passport for Nadia too, Dad, in case she needs one," Grace said still believing that Nadia was safe, and would be found alive and well.

"Call Jamila and set up a meeting somewhere busy in the Mall of Emirates. It's close to the sailing club," Rita suggested.

Grace called her immediately and arranged the lunch meeting for the next day.

Chapter Eleven

At breakfast the next day in their hotel rooms, Grace couldn't eat. She felt sick with fear of failing to get Darcy to safety and ending up back in jail for life. She put on a brave face and mentally prepared for the ordeal ahead, hiding her fear to her parents.

Her parents checked out of the hotel and left for the airport with instructions for their next meeting. Jonathan, Grace's brother, called and offered to help.

"Hi Jonathan, will you get a new sim card for me and give it to Mother please? They're on their way home to get passports and visas before flying to India to meet us, it'd be great if you could." Grace asked him.

"Consider it done. I'm still in shock as to what's gone on over there. Please get out now and come back safe together."

Rita took Grace and her belongings to the safehouse on Jumeirah Beach Road near to the Dubai offshore sailing club, where they stopped off to meet Captain Lincoln and his lovely wife Jenny.

Lincoln conveyed the procedure and introduced Grace to Barney, the man who was to drive her and Darcy the next day after lunch with Jamila. He knew the fastest route back to the sailing club avoiding CCTV security cameras.

Grace, mentally exhausted but pumped up with adrenaline, dropped off her suitcases in a bedroom at the large sparsely furnished safehouse.

"I can't thank you enough for what you've done for me, Rita. I'm forever indebted to you." Grace reached out to embrace her.

"Hey, it's my job and you're another satisfied client to relay to new clients who can find solace. So, you'd better be ready for success tomorrow." Rita smiled as she accepted Grace's embrace.

Grace released her hug and smiled back. "I like your modesty, and confidence of my successful task ahead. Thank you."

Rita nodded. "Go ahead and use anything from the stores that you need for your trip."

"Thanks again and see you upon my return here." Grace waved goodbye at the door.

She made herself a fresh coffee in the newly furbished kitchen, before looking around the house for what she needed for the next day. After packing a small bag containing a change of clothes for her and Darcy, she found a full black abaya from the house storeroom, much needed for the disguised getaway.

The day was drawing into evening and the house inside became dark. She instantly felt alone again, not prison cell alone but alone inside this time, a feeling that she'd never felt before, with the wanting for all of this to be over. To be back home in safety with her family.

*   *   *

The next day, Grace took a local taxi to the mall with Barney following behind in his car.

She met a worried-looking Jamila at the French café. Darcy was waiting impatiently to see her.

He ran towards Grace. She picked him up and swung him round, kissed and embraced him tightly. She didn't want to let go.

She wanted to take him back to the hotel pool and enjoy the rest of their holiday, but it wasn't a holiday anymore. Grace's life had turned upside down and she was about to break the law for the first time ever. Going against all her values, but her family came first and she would do what needed to be done to secure their safety.

"Where have you been, Mom, and where is Momma?" Darcy asked.

"We've been doing some legal work here. It was unexpected. I'm so sorry to leave you without us." She hugged him tighter and hid her face away as she struggled to hold back tears.

They sat and ordered lunch as the kids chatted about having ice cream afterwards.

"Where's Nadia?" Grace asked Jamila.

Jamila bent her head avoiding eye contact. "I don't know."

"Come on, Jamila, I know you know where she is.

Tell me please. I'm leaving for London this evening and need to know she's safe."

"I can only tell you that she is safe but I haven't seen her since Friday morning, when my parents took her in a helicopter to a clinical facility in the desert to help her to remember who she is."

"What? What do you mean a clinical facility?" Grace raised her voice as diners stared in their direction.

"It's a place where parents send mentally ill women to get treatment."

"Nadia isn't mentally ill and you know it! How can this be legal? They can't commit her to a facility without evidence of instability."

"The law here states that she is mentally ill for wanting to be with a woman instead of a man. It's not normal in this country, you know that. My parents believe it will make her normal if she receives treatment." Jamila's eyes were filling up with tears.

"Oh, Jamila, what have they done? Where is this facility?" Grace whispered the words that she couldn't believe she was uttering.

"I don't know the exact location it's somewhere far out in the desert. Nadia was drugged after trying to escape jumping from the car, before they got her to the private helicopter pad."

Grace felt a wave of sickness and rushed to the washroom to throw up.

Wiping her face with a paper towel, she pulled herself together. Holding on to the sink, Grace rang Rita to give her the news of Nadia's situation.

Hidden Evil

"Do you know where this place is?" Grace asked.

"Yes, but it's not easy to get to. There's no road access, it was built in secret by wealthy families to offer solutions for women who disobey the orders of their family, religion or their husbands. It's a costly, lavish facility with highly trained psychotherapists, who focus on emotional and personality problems. A practice of unethical and harmful therapy, exacerbating anxiety and self-hatred for those treated for what is not a mental disorder."

"Oh god. How bad can it get for her?"

"Listen, Grace, she's alive so there's hope. I've heard they sometimes use electroconvulsive shock therapy to erase memory, which is a side effect of the treatment, amongst other medical horrors that take place there. It's not a recognised mainstream facility, so it can't be considered a viable treatment if the law can't admit same-sex attraction exists, can it!" Rita told her gently.

"I must get her out of there. Can you find someone to help me?"

"You get Darcy out to safety first and I'll execute a rescue plan for Nadia."

The bustle of the shoppers and other guests in the shopping mall café went unnoticed as Grace walked slowly back, dazed, to the table where Darcy was happily eating ice cream and laughing with the girls.

Grace's hands trembled as she sipped water from her glass, placed it down and with precision knocked it deliberately over, so the water would fall onto Darcy's jeans.

"Oops sorry, sweetheart, that was clumsy of me. Finish your ice cream and I'll get you dried off in the washroom when you've finished. We don't want you walking around in wet jeans." Grace smiled at him hiding her nerves.

"I'm ready to dry them now, Mom, I've finished." He stood and smiled.

Grace took her backpack from the chair next to hers and walked down to the washrooms holding Darcy's hand to guide him.

* * *

Once inside she pulled him into the disabled cubicle, so she could more easily change his clothes and put a cap on him. It took her three attempts to wrap the abaya around herself and fix the head dress to cover her head and face. She hadn't done it before and realised that it was not as easy as she thought it would be and her nervous disposition wasn't helping.

She felt panic as each attempt failed but hid it well from Darcy as she eventually succeeded. He stared at her.

She sat on the toilet and held his arms with both hands, focused on his eyes to give him full instructions of the next move.

"I need you to listen carefully. Let's play a game of hide and seek by walking from here without Jamila or the girls spotting us. We'll go straight down the escalator to my friend Barney who will take us for a boat ride and hide in a cabin out in the sea. Okay?"

Darcy nodded and clapped.

She grabbed his hand and walked towards the escalator with her head facing towards Jamila and her girls, sitting at the table enjoying their ice cream. Jamila was chatting to her girls and did not look up to see Grace pass by as they slipped away unnoticed.

The mall was packed with tourists of all nationalities, dressed in various casual and smart outfits. Many other women were dressed in full abayas and hijabs, some with full face coverings showing marital status.

Grace blended in neatly.

Nothing out of the ordinary on an average day at Emirates Mall.

Chapter Twelve

Once down the escalators, Grace turned and pushed the sliding doors outside where Barney was waiting in a line of other cars. She walked casually to his car instantly feeling the humidity outside. She opened the door and sat in the back with Darcy in the airconditioned car and pleasantly introduced them, holding back her panic of being followed.

"When we get near to the sailing club you need to take off your abaya. Women in traditional dress aren't allowed in the club as it's licenced for alcohol," Barney instructed her in his New Zealand accent.

Captain Lincoln had registered them under false names as guests on the security desk when they arrived. Barney gave their names and paid the small fee to enter the private club again.

Grace's heart raced as her stomach tightened. She held onto Darcy, smiling at the security guard next to the barrier.

Barney parked up without hurry in the small car

park near the front of the restaurant as if he had done this procedure many times and knew how to not appear conspicuous towards the nosey guards.

Darcy pointed to a large yacht. "Are we going on that big boat, Mom?"

"Barney will show us which one we're going to hide on so Jamila and the girls won't find us. It's going to be a very exciting game." Grace smiled as the knots in her belly tightened but were ignored.

Barney boldly led them past the large crowded restaurant with outside seats under umbrella-shaded tables and electric fans swirling cold water into the air to soothe away the sweltering heat, which made Grace sweat more intensely.

They walked down the boardwalk passing dozens of different sized sailboats. Employed expatriates were drinking alcohol and chatting, some boats played low music and others were in the middle of a fully operational party.

They arrived at Captain Lincoln's fifty-foot white catamaran. He was sitting on deck drinking a beer with Jenny when he spotted them. He stood and beamed a smile as he held out his hands to help them aboard.

"You must be Darcy," Jenny said in her southern English accent as she held out her hand to shake it, offering him a huge smile.

"Yes, what's your name?" Darcy politely asked her. He shook her hand.

"I'm Jenny and I'm going to help you to hide under the bed downstairs." She winked at him.

Once the introductions were done, Barney exited

the boat and removed the ropes to free it from the dock. Waving goodbye, he beamed a smile back at them.

Jenny took Grace and Darcy down to the cabin and showed them where to hide. She gave them both a drink of water and joined Lincoln up on deck to get ready to sail to India.

She pulled in the fenders from each side and waited for instructions from her husband to set up the sail.

Lincoln turned on the engine and stood at the helm, slowly guiding his boat out of the dock into the open gulf.

He instructed Jenny to get ready to pull up the sails as he set the course and came to help her.

Grace noticed from below deck how skilfully they worked harmoniously and manoeuvred the boat out, feeling safe in their capable hands.

"Grace, you can come up on deck now it's safe," Lincoln called down to her.

"They won't find us now, Mom, will they?" Darcy said.

"I hope we can enjoy our lovely sail on the ocean before they know where we are," Grace said holding him next to her as she turned to look at Lincoln seeking reassurance.

"We're not in the clear yet, Darcy. Why don't you keep an eye out for them over there." Lincoln pointed towards the dock where they'd sailed from and gave him his sailor's cap.

Darcy stood watching the crowded boats of people and the shoreline fade into the distance.

Jenny took out her hamper full of icicles and offered one to Darcy. She poured a gin and tonic for Grace and herself as Lincoln lit his cigar and drank a beer. The boat sailed smoothly under the blazing sun as they sat around the shaded table at the front of the deck in the sea breeze.

* * *

An hour later into the ocean they heard the sound of a helicopter and a boat moving swiftly towards them. Lincoln stood up looking shocked.

"Get them down in the hatch quickly," he told Jenny.

Grace grabbed hold of Darcy with shaking hands as Jenny led them downstairs and lifted up the cabin bed and removed the wooden insert.

"Get inside and stay still and quiet," Jenny instructed sternly as she replaced the wooden insert and pulled the mattress tight. She smoothed the sheets and quilt over it as Grace and Darcy lay together in the darkness.

Jenny sat on the chair next to the bed and started sewing a garment surrounded by fabric on top of the bed in an attempt to appear busy.

Chapter Thirteen

Grace lay still, her hands trembling as she gripped onto little Darcy. Gently holding her hand over his mouth in the darkness of the hidden void under the bed.

She swallowed the bile to the back of her throat and held her breath silent. She couldn't hear Captain Lincoln but the smell of his cigar smoke reassured her that he was near.

Her legs were numb, curled with her knees bent in the small space as her son lay still between them, but that was the least of her troubles.

A loud helicopter hovered over the sailboat. The coastguards' boots thumped as a team of guards boarded the deck from their military vessel.

"Where is the boy?" a uniformed Emirate guard asked in broken English.

Captain Lincoln stared at him. Wiping his grey

hair from his wrinkled sun-drenched face with his cigar in his fingers. "What boy?"

"A boy has been abducted from his auntie this afternoon. He is the grandson of our General Mohammed Aktoum and he believes the boy is being smuggled out on a boat from here."

"Not on my boat, sir." Lincoln gestured for them to look around.

The guards became impatient as they searched the boat for stowaways. Finding Jenny alone in a cabin quietly sewing, one of the guards politely apologised for the intrusion and departed.

The small team of guards continued searching the boat inside and out before feeling satisfied that a boy was not to be found. They left empty handed after another apology to Lincoln for their intrusion.

"That was a close call," Jenny said to Lincoln as she appeared up on deck moments later. "I had no idea this boy was related to the General!"

"I didn't want to worry you unnecessarily, did I, darling." Lincoln winked at her as she tapped his arm and smiled at his audacity.

They sailed freely on to India without any further disruptions.

* * *

Grace put on a brave face for Darcy but all she could think about was Nadia in a secret illegal sanitorium alone and scared.

Chapter Fourteen

In the desert secret sanatorium sat a medicated Nadia, perplexed and alone, in her padded white cell, strapped in a straitjacket.

That wonderful Friday morning when she had woken with a cup of tea, from the mother whom she cherished, seemed a lifetime ago. Nadia had showered and dressed in her abaya, excited to accompany both her sister and mother to Friday prayers.

By the time she sat in the car she felt disparate. A drowsy dizzy feeling overwhelmed her. She saw her father step into the driving seat replacing the family driver, which was unusual as he should already be at the mosque, arriving in his own car.

Her father drove down Emirates Road towards the Al Maktoum International Airport where a helicopter awaited.

"Where are we going, Father? This isn't the way to our mosque," Nadia asked still feeling drowsy.

"What's wrong with Nadia, why is she slurring?" Jamila asked her mother.

"We are going to save your sister from herself," her mother answered, muttering prayers, asking for forgiveness.

Nadia widened her heavy eyes as the car stopped and she saw a helicopter in the distance and two men running towards the car. Their father signalled for them to take her into the helicopter.

"I'm not getting in there. Where are they taking me?" Nadia shouted, jumped out the car and ran back towards the highway.

"They are taking you somewhere safe to make you well again. I want my daughter back with me. Not in London with a woman who has shamed our family." Fatima growled loudly towards her in the distance.

Nadia was on the floor, kicking two men who were lifting her up. She struggled intensely and attempted to rescue herself from their grasp, but one of the men stuck a syringe in her neck, which knocked her out. She almost fell back to the ground in the sand as they grabbed each arm and carried her almost lifeless into the waiting helicopter.

* * *

"Where is she going?" Jamila asked with tears in her eyes after witnessing her sister being abducted by her father's collaborators.

"Stop crying she's going to a clinic in the desert where she'll receive treatment to be herself again. It's safe and highly recommended by a friend of your father's, who took their daughter there last year," Fatima assured her.

The helicopter flew off into the desert with Nadia and the two men as their father drove Fatima and Jamila in silence to the mosque for Friday prayers.

Jamila stopped crying. She was in complete shock to see her loving parents willing to do anything to bring Nadia back to live with them again.

Jamila never thought they'd go to such lengths and became afraid for Nadia and what might happen to her in this secret illegal mental health clinic.

Chapter Fifteen

The helicopter set down on the helipad outside a large white-glassed contemporary building. Set in manicured grounds of greenery, tropical plants and dozens of colourful flowers, it was a surreal idyllic setting.

The medics appeared with a stretcher to take Nadia inside, who remained unconscious from the injection. The large high ceilings were set with windows of smoked glass, keeping out the desert sun. Vast corridors ran endlessly through it.

The female nurses removed Nadia's abaya and all her underclothing, dressed her in a white jumpsuit and placed her in a straitjacket. They lay her down on a bed and cuffed her to the bedrail so she couldn't attempt escape upon waking. They turned the lights out and left her alone in the air-conditioned sterile room.

* * *

Nadia woke in the dark and felt the taste of the injection in her dry mouth. Her muscles ached as her belly rumbled for food. She felt cold and smelled of a mix of medication and disinfectant.

Where the fuck am I?

She began to remember earlier in the car with her family and the helicopter.

"Get me out of here! Get me out of here!" She shouted louder and louder, feeling scared and angry.

A nurse quietly entered and switched on a light, carrying a tray of food and drink.

"Good evening, Miss Aktoum. Can you try to sit up please?" She spoke sternly in a Johannesburg accent as she walked towards her and gestured for her to sit up as she placed the tray on a nearby movable stand and dragged it over to the bed.

"Where the fuck am I? Why am I here?" Nadia shouted.

"Your parents have sent you here for various medical and psychological treatments. We'd prefer it if you do not use foul language and try to keep some form of decorum. I know it's a surprise for you to be here but being polite isn't hard is it?"

"A surprise? I'm shocked. What am I supposed to say when I wake up unable to move, cuffed to the bed in darkness, no idea where I am or why I'm here?"

"Well, now you know, try to be polite. We are here under instructions from your parents to keep you safe, and medicate you if we feel the need to."

"Medicate me! How?"

"If you try to harm yourself or attempt escape then

we will medicate you so you won't be able to move freely. It's in your best interest to co-operate with us." The nurse sounded like she was reading a script of rules.

Another nurse entered the room and sat silently beside the bed stirring a soupy substance in a dish, ready to feed her as she lifted up a cup of water for her to sip first. Nadia sensed that she was gentle, unlike the first sarcastic nurse.

Nadia felt exhausted, confused and angry, with extreme thirst as she sipped on the water offered and began to monitor her situation, observing both nurses and her cold environment.

She knew she needed to keep herself hydrated and alert to enable her eventual escape from this hell. She decided to use her wits and get friendly with the kind nurse, hoping she might become her aid, ignoring the other nurse as she left the room.

"What perfume are you wearing? It's a pleasant fragrance," Nadia asked.

"It's one of those that you create yourself at the fragrance store in Dubai Mall. My husband bought it for me but I chose the ingredients. It's not expensive and I think it's nice to have your own individual scent, don't you?"

"I agree and it suits your kindness," Nadia grovelled.

"Thank you." The nurse looked up at Nadia through her spectacles, clearly not used to compliments from new angry patients, forcing a smile as she began to feed her mouthfuls of soup and bread.

"Where is this place?" Nadia asked her.

"It's in the middle of the desert. I don't know exactly as they bring me in from the airfield near Al Maktoum International Airport by helicopter to do my shifts. I live here five days on and five days off to go home to be with my family."

"That must be tough on you, leaving your family. Do you have kids?"

"It's difficult sometimes to leave my boys but my husband is there in the evenings and they are taken care of by my mother who lives with us, so it's not so bad and the salary is excellent, better than the other private hospitals in Dubai."

"Where are you from? How long have you been here?"

"Cape Town is our home but we both have great careers here. My husband's a doctor. We decided to uproot and move here five years ago, we have no regrets."

"Sounds perfect for you both. I'm glad you're happy."

"Thank you. I can see we're going to get along whilst you're here getting your treatment."

"What treatments are you talking about?"

"The psychologist will give you that information tomorrow. I have no idea why you're here, you seem okay to me."

"A psychologist? This is a mental health facility?"

"Yes, it's mainly for teenage girls and younger women with personality disorders."

"What treatments do the young women receive?"

"Various. They're always angry when they arrive but they settle in once they undergo their specific treatments and emotional counselling."

"How long do they usually stay for?"

"That depends on the person and how well they take to the treatments, it can be weeks or even months to get well. Some women, the stubborn ones, stay much longer than the others."

"There's nothing wrong with me. I'm not a kid, I'm a thirty-year-old woman. They can't keep me here against my will. You can see that, can't you?"

"You do seem fine but it's not my job to question the specialists in here or your parents who have admitted you. I only take care of the nursing side of things, keep your prescribed medication stable and keep you safe from harming yourself."

"Can you remove these cuffs and take this jacket off me please? I feel like a prisoner with these on."

"I can't, sorry. That's the psychologist's job. They determine when it's safe to remove them."

Nadia finished by swallowing the date cake which she despised as the nurse packed up to get ready to leave her alone again.

"Can you leave the light on please? I don't like it dark."

"Sorry, I have to turn it off and close the door. It's the rule for newbies. Try to get a good sleep and I'll be back bright and early with your breakfast. G-night."

Nadia lay with her eyes wide, full of despair, as she tried to digest the situation her parents had placed her.

She didn't know that Grace was in a filthy jail cell accused of her disappearance and possible murder.

Nadia had no idea what her parents planned for her as she wept herself to sleep, feeling hopelessly shackled in darkness.

Chapter Sixteen

As Captain Lincoln and Jenny pulled safely into the small boats dock at Mumbai, Grace felt rested and delighted that Darcy was safe but remained extremely anxious about Nadia's health and her whereabouts.

The phone lines and internet connections were not steady at sea and the only messages she received via radio were updates from her parents and that Nadia still hadn't been found, but Rita had her team searching for the facility in the desert.

Grace and Darcy went ashore and saw her parents waiting to greet them. Darcy ran towards them and Grace was instantly relieved to see their smiling faces.

"How are you, Gracie, and how are you, Darcy?" Robert asked as he embraced them tightly.

"We're good, Dad, but I'm worried about Nadia, her parents have taken her to an illegal private mental health clinic somewhere in the desert. They drugged her to knock her out and put her into a helicopter.

"They've meticulously planned everything. I'd bet

her mother lied about having cancer, just to get us over to Dubai, then got me arrested out of the way, so they could commit her to a mental institution. You know what that means don't you? Them believing she has a mental illness for being a lesbian. Thinking that it can be erased with electric shock treatment." Grace paused and bit her lip to stop herself from crying.

"I can't believe her parents could be so cruel to do what they've done to you both." Robert hugged her again as she kept tears inside.

"I'm so sorry, Gracie," Susan said. "You always knew that her parents have old-fashioned views and wouldn't understand or accept you into their family. They would've attended your wedding if they could accept it. Their religious beliefs and the UAE law makes it impossible for them to comprehend, but you're right; it's shameful. How could they do this to their own flesh and blood?" Susan embraced her again.

"I need to get back to Dubai as fast as the boat can take me," Grace said.

They sat at the port side for a few minutes whilst Captain Lincoln went off to sort out their passport stamps and explain to one of the officials, an old friend who helped him to rescue innocent people, that only Darcy would be entering the port that day.

A visit visa from the Indian embassy was already in Darcy's new passport and it had needed an entry stamp to get him legally back on the plane departure home to Heathrow with his grandparents.

"All set and ready to go." Lincoln smiled as he returned their passports.

"I'll call you when I reach Dubai from the new sim card," Grace said, taking it from her mother with Nadia's new passport. Susan took Darcy by the hand.

"I can't use my old number as Nadia's father might be monitoring my movements. I need to stay incognito for as long as possible. I love you both. I love you, Darcy." She embraced them, no longer holding back the tears, before boarding the boat as they waved her goodbye.

As the boat set sail, Grace had a sudden overwhelming urge to get off and go home with them to safety but resisted the urge. She would not go anywhere without Nadia, under any circumstances, even though Grace was secretly terrified of the consequences of what she had done and was about to do to get her wife out safely.

Grace waved frantically until they were out of sight. She sat on the deck, relieved that one part of her horrendous fight was over. Darcy was safe and on his way home with her parents. Mohammed had no idea of their whereabouts. She had outsmarted a corrupt imbecile and felt very proud of herself.

"Let's get straight back on the wide ocean and we can have a drink to calm our nerves." Lincoln smiled at the successful rescue that they had left behind.

"That sounds like a good plan." Grace had to stop herself from raging inside and helped them get the boat out to sea. She had missed sailing and enjoyed the company of her seasoned Captain Lincoln and his crew wife Jenny.

The morning sun shined brightly as they left port, lifting up the fenders and releasing the sails at the mast.

Afterwards they sat at the deck table and drank gin and tonics, Lincoln lit a cigar and put his feet up to drink his beer with the wind behind them.

This could've been one of the most delightful trips we ever had, if only Nadia was safe in my arms sitting sipping drinks with us on this deck.

"Nadia loves to sail too. We went around the islands of Thailand on our honeymoon seven years ago," Grace said tapping her glass.

Jenny squeezed Grace's hand. "You'll get to sail together again soon."

"I'll drink to that, ladies. Cheers," Lincoln piped in as he clinked his bottle on their glasses.

Chapter Seventeen

The following morning the kind nurse entered the room. Nadia already awake sobbing. The nurse wiped away the tears and helped her to sit up ready for breakfast.

"Come on now, don't be sad. You'll soon be out of here and on with your life. Let's get you fed and watered."

Nadia ate breakfast finding it difficult to swallow, her throat was tight and sore from crying most of the night shackled in her bed. She had since managed to digest what her parents had done to her, by taking control of her life in such an evil way.

Instinctively knowing that it was her mother who had wanted this abduction more than her doting father, who always agreed and went along with her mother's wishes.

I'll never forgive my mother for this, NEVER!

After breakfast the nurse uncuffed Nadia from the

bed and helped her stand and sit into a blue wheelchair, her straitjacket remained fixed in place.

"I can walk. I don't need to sit in a chair."

"It's the rules. You have to go in the chair so I can wheel you in and out of the clinic for your first consultation. The psychologist will decide if you can walk or not, after he has seen you."

Nadia sat despondent in the chair as the nurse wheeled her along vast corridors to get to the therapist's room. Nadia not only felt alone but it seemed like she was the only person in this huge building. She couldn't hear or see another soul anywhere. There were no doctors, nurses or patients. It was empty on the route she took to the therapy room.

They arrived at a large white carpeted room with white leather Le Corbusier chairs and a matching long white chaise longue on one side. A white-coated doctor sat at his desk awaiting her arrival. He looked up and greeted her politely.

"Good morning Miss Aktoum, how are you feeling today? I'm Doctor Hancock, it's a pleasure to meet you," he said in his upper-class English accent.

"Are you my therapist?"

"Not really, I like to think of myself as your eminent psychologist."

"Then don't ask me how I'm feeling because I definitely don't need a psychologist."

Nadia looked out of the window and ignored his presence.

"Now let's not get off to a bad start. It's important that you trust me so I can help you."

Hidden Evil

"What help do you think I need?"

"I have my records here stating that you are married to a woman in London of which your parents disapprove. My job is to help you understand that your choice is due to a mental disorder and I aim to reverse your desire to choose women over men in intimate relationships."

Nadia burst out laughing and held her head back as she howled louder in his direction.

He shifted in his seat.

"Best of luck with that, where shall we start?" She continued to laugh at him.

"Will you lie on the sofa please?" he asked nervously.

"Take this jacket off me first, sadist."

"I can't do that before I've made an assessment of your compliance to change." He spoke quietly as if to relax her.

"I'm not complying to anything of the sort. Let me out of this hellhole."

"I can see you're stubborn so I'll start with your first treatment today. I'm the expert in this facility and there's no time like the present to prepare you for exit. I'll show you how I change the way you think and who you think you are." He aggressively wheeled her to the next room.

Inside the freezing cold room stood two men and two women wearing white overalls, green plastic gloves and matching green hairnets.

Next to a long brown tubular machine positioned from the ceiling in the middle of the room were computers and wires attached to a long slim bed with leather straps draped across it.

"Oh my god, no. Let me out of here!" Nadia screamed as she struggled violently to free herself from the jacket and fell onto the marbled floor out of the wheelchair.

"Prepare her for the first round of ECT," Doctor Hancock ordered.

The two men lifted Nadia off the floor kicking and screaming.

"Please don't do this to me. I don't need any of this. I'm not mentally ill." The stark reality of what was going to happen to her was finally understood, why she was in the prison clinic and what she was there for. She carried on struggling, terrified, but knowing her struggle was useless.

The men slammed her onto the bed, strapping her down.

A woman pushed a plastic bite block into Nadia's mouth securing it in place.

She could no longer scream or move. She lay defenceless, trembling in a nightmarish dream, whilst the other woman wiped transmission gel ready to attach the wires through plastic stickers onto her head.

* * *

Doctor Hancock administered a muscle-relaxing anaesthetic ensuring that the first seizure was mildly activated to cause maximum memory loss whilst alleviating any depression.

Hidden Evil

"We are rebooting your cognitive and norepinephrine levels and restoring your neuro-connections that reconnect your nerves and increase your dopamine and serotonin to remove your depression." He stared into her terrified eyes as she blinked in fear of the unknown.

The female nurse attached the wires meticulously onto the areas around Nadia's head. Doctor Hancock pressed the button on the machine as they all stood back and watched Nadia's limp body rise into the air and back down onto the bed, aided by electricity across her membrane.

"That should be enough for her first round," Doctor Hancock assured himself proudly.

Afterwards her limp body was moved onto a stretcher wheeled to her room where the men lifted her onto her bed and adjusted the straitjacket to obtain maximum lack of movement as she lay in a deep catatonic state.

My heartbeat feels as though it's in the base of my throat, void of noise. My mouth is dry, it hurts to swallow. I roll on my side, my face turned towards the long window. The bright light hurts my eyes. I can't use my hands to touch my eyes to remove the aching. I turn back to the door. My lids remain heavy and my head hurts from the thumping inside my brain.

What's happened to my brain? I fidget and feel my heart pounding. I go back to sleep again until the sound of screaming jolts me back awake, but then I realise that the noise was in my head, locked somewhere in a nightmare dream.

My body aches and I am breathless like I've been running, but I'm still lying on my back unable to move freely with the straitjacket tucked up tight. All I want to do is curl into a foetal position and not be here.

Who am I? How can I know all this yet not my name?

Something is wrong, where am I? I know I'm somewhere strange on a hard mattress that's not mine with sheets like a hospital bed.

I have a sensation of being elevated so I open my eyes. The lights are bright fluorescent white.

I remember the curly-haired man in white telling me something. What was it? Was he smiling at me or sneering? Something unpleasant happened to me. What was it?

I feel sick in my belly and my body begins to ache more all over. I wait for the memory to surface. It's not coming to me!

I smell the nurse's perfume and then it hits me, like a wave of dread.

I'm in a prison clinic where they're trying to make me lose my memory. It's working because I can't remember who I am.

I turn and face down in my bed. It's hard because the straitjacket is still on but at least the handcuffs are gone. My throat starts to close because I want to cry again, but crying isn't the answer, it's not going to get me out of here.

"Good morning, Miss Aktoum, how are you feeling today?"

"Like I've been abducted and forced to go along with my mother's wishes to cure me of something that can't be cured."

"I don't think the doctors are trying to cure you, miss, just make you feel normal like everyone else."

The nurse helped her to sit up and offered a drink of warm tea to help soothe her throat and quench her thirst. The liquid went down slowly and burned her throat.

"What day is it?"

"Monday."

"Really? I've missed a whole day. What happened? What will they do to me today?"

"I have instructions to leave you to rest all day and allow the treatment to work, ready for the next round tomorrow."

The nurse left with the half-eaten eggs on toasted bread, leaving Nadia alone with the smell of perfume in the air. It was a delightful smell of freshly cut flowers which reminded her of Grace, who Nadia still remembered.

And then the tears came.

Chapter Eighteen

I'm never going to forget who I am. They are delusional if they think for one moment this horrific invasion of my body and brain will make any difference to my mind and how much I love Grace, Darcy and our wonderful life together in London.

I'm never going to forget the day we met at Oxford when she was playing chess. I'm never going to forget our first few dates at the local café and then at the restaurant on the corner.

I'm never going to forget our wedding day in London, with all our friends and Grace's adorable parents. How kind and understanding they are, how they want her to be happy and live her life to the full. How supportive they have been and how they love me too.

How lucky I am to have them in my life as surrogate parents. I should have been happy enough with all that. I should have ignored the void not having my own parents in my life and them not accepting of who I am.

I'm never going to forget our amazing honeymoon sailing around the islands of Thailand and how Grace taught me to become a competent sailor, just like her father had taught her as a teenager when they sailed regularly off the coast of England to the Isle of Wight.

I'm never going to forget how we wanted a baby. How my brother-in-law Jonathan delighted in helping us to conceive with his donation of sperm, so that Grace could be related and feel closer to our baby.

I'm never going to forget those long evenings that summer when Darcy came into our lives. How we adored every moment we shared together. I'm never going to forget the love and tenderness I feel in Grace's arms and when hugging Darcy.

I'm never ever going to forget who I am.

Never…

Nadia drifted off to sleep in oblivion still trembling from the effects of her first treatment and wondering where Grace and Darcy were. Were they safe or had her parents abducted them too?

Next morning the nurse woke her and the same routine followed as it did every other day for two weeks. The ECT treatments became more intense with higher voltage, leading to her becoming more and more withdrawn each time and resulting in the removal of her straitjacket.

Nadia no longer resisted and was ready after seven sessions, for emotional psychiatric therapy, where she lay on the sofa and answered questions from the therapist.

The answers Doctor Hancock expected to hear eventually came. The effects of ECT had worked its magic and she had become a perfect patient, ready to be indoctrinated into a new emotional level of self-worth, taking her meals in the dining area and sitting reading the Quran in the day room between meals.

Chapter Nineteen

Nadia began to notice other patients who all looked docile like herself, sitting reading the Quran or walking around slowly looking into the air. Aisha a skinny young woman with heavily dilated pupils constantly mumbled to herself.

Aisha wasn't docile though, she was just quiet. She would look up from time to time and watch the others. She feared nothing and Nadia wondered why she was there. She would follow other patients around with her eyes watching them without moving her head.

Nadia decided to strike up a conversation with Aisha and find out why she was there and attempt to alleviate her own horrific experiences.

"Hello how are you doing today?" Nadia said, sounding genuine.

"Terrible," Aisha replied then looked away from her.

"I'm sorry to hear that. Is there anything I can do for you?"

"Sure, go find my mother and put a bullet in her brain." Aisha chuckled loudly.

Nadia was taken aback by her comments. She felt scared because the look in her eyes made her realise that she was serious.

"What did she do?" Nadia asked half fearing the answer but half wanting to know.

"She hates me and told me I was too crazy to have a baby." Aisha put her head into her hands and sobbed.

The Johannesburg nurse came over and took Aisha firmly back to her room as she turned around to Nadia with pleading eyes.

The next day Nadia heard the familiar mumblings from Aisha, she couldn't make out the whole sentence but it sounded like she was saying 'kill my mother'.

"Aisha doesn't want to read the Quran today Aisha wants to kill her mother." She spoke out loud in the third person conversing with herself and moved her head without moving her eyes then she froze and stopped breathing, her cold eyes glaring.

Nadia stared at her, waiting for her to go back to normal as their eyes met but Aisha looked unconscious. Eventually Aisha began to breathe again as two nurses placed her still frozen into a wheelchair and wheeled her back to her room before returning to the day room.

"What the hell's just happened to her, why did she freeze like that? I've never seen anyone or any living thing freeze that way," Nadia asked the gentle nurse from Cape Town.

"She's a delicate young woman gone crazy and the doctors are trying an experiment. I'm heartbroken watching over her, but she is a severe case and the doctors know what they're doing. When she says she wants to kill her mother she gets so stressed it makes the medication freeze her.

"The extensive shock therapy seemed to have messed up her nerves so badly that when she stresses, she acts like she's getting shocked again. She tenses up, stops breathing and sometimes passes out, but her nerves keep firing so she's still with us. She's okay. When she comes around, she forgets about killing her mother and remains calm. Until the next time."

"That freaks me out. How can you deal with a woman who acts like that? Surely you know what they're doing here is wrong, it's inhumane. What sort of principles do you have working here with these quacks?"

"We nurses only take care of patients and help them recover, we don't make the choices of what type of medical treatment they receive. The doctors always cure everyone eventually and the women go home fixed." The nurse replied without eye contact, as if knowing she was working with psychopaths experimenting on young women for financial gain.

Nadia persevered. "Why does she want to kill her mother? Where's her baby?"

"She's not well enough to have a baby so her

mother brought her here to fix that. Since the termination she's getting worse."

"What do mean? It's not permitted to terminate in this country."

"Why do you think they brought her here to this private clinic?" the nurse whispered.

What horrors are taking place here. I can't believe this. I need to get out of here fast before I start saying I want to kill my mother for bringing me here.

Nadia decided to go and check on Aisha, feeling appalled by the experiments taking place on such a fragile woman. Nadia entered the brightly lit florescent white room identical to her own. Aisha was sitting on her bed in a daze as Nadia closed the door behind her.

"Hello, Aisha. I've come to check on you. Are you feeling alright?" Nadia said quietly.

"No, Aisha doesn't like noise… shush." She stood and placed her hand on Nadia's mouth then gripped her arm.

Nadia slowly removed Aisha's hand from her mouth. "Please keep a safe distance, Aisha, remember my personal space."

Aisha moved away from her then moved her own body in a circle motion like a little girl, her eyes focused, piercing into Nadia's frightened eyes.

"My personal space, my personal space," Aisha repeated in a mimicking singing voice.

Then she stopped and with her head cocked to one side her eyes stared into Nadia's again. Nadia was terrified.

Hidden Evil

Aisha spoke in a lower deeper and darker tone. "You are in MY space."

The only thing that Nadia heard was the usage of the word 'my'. She trembled as Aisha grabbed her throat and started choking her. Squeezing her hands tighter and tighter around her neck, making Nadia gag for breath.

Nadia pushed her off, trying not to look scared. She tried to reason with her. "That's not okay, Aisha. Stop it."

Aisha threw herself to the floor, moaning, her long dark hair covering her face. She made whiny sounds as if she was crying.

Nadia looked at the closed door behind her. Panicked, she decided to make a run for it.

Aisha flipped herself round and stood up, running towards Nadia, screaming and howling. Her face was contorted and was no longer the gentle muttering Aisha that Nadia had seen over the last few days in the day room, silently reading the Quran.

Aisha pushed her face into hers with a grip on her arm so strong Nadia couldn't move. Aisha looked positively inhuman. Nadia fought her for control, then Aisha bit her arm as hard as she could like a dog fighting off torture.

Nadia screamed which started a chorus of screams from other nearby rooms. She struggled to release her arm as she felt the pain from Aisha's teeth tearing into it again. Blood covered Nadia's sleeve.

Nadia yelled out in pain. "Aisha, stop it, you're hurting me. I'm not your mother."

Aisha let go of her arm and looked at the blood as she moved away and began to sob.

"If you hadn't hurt Aisha, she wouldn't hurt you," Aisha said in yet another squeaky voice.

Nadia didn't know what to say as she stood holding her arm.

She was done playing nice with this crazy woman who was changing from one person to another.

Finally, the door opened. It was the nurse from Johannesburg.

Aisha flipped herself around again and the contorted look reappeared on her face. She leaped straight at the nurse, her mouth on the woman's face and bit hard as she clawed at her and bit again and again.

The nurse screamed whilst Nadia watched in a daze. Her head was swimming as she began to feel weak from loss of blood. A male guard appeared so Aisha let go of the nurse and ran off into the halls, screeching like a banshee.

Nadia, shocked and trembling, vomited as she looked at the nurse lying on the floor, her face covered in blood, as if a ravenous wolf had eaten it.

The guard ran off after Aisha and left them both in the room.

* * *

After a few seconds a crowd of doctors and nurses entered the room, placed the nurse onto a stretcher and into a helicopter for hospital care. She never came back to work again. Nobody missed her sarcasm or lack of compassion.

Nadia, still trembling, was placed into a wheelchair and wheeled towards the medicine room to bathe and bandage her arm. She saw Aisha sitting in a corner with a crowd of doctors and security men around her. Some of them were keeping their distance from her because she had a knife.

"Get back get back from my baby!" Aisha screamed, waving the knife around, not allowing anyone to get near her.

Everyone stood still waiting for a chance to pounce on her and grab the knife.

"Oh god it's coming... get a midwife, get a midwife now the baby's coming." The knife went down and she put her hand on her belly, this time her voice was quiet and almost sweet.

The security men tried closing in but the screaming came back and the knife went up again, waving above her head.

"You bastards come any closer and I'll gut all of you," she howled.

The sweet voice came back again. "It won't come out, my baby won't come out."

"Where's my baby, where's my baby?" Aisha screamed and slid the knife into her belly, moving it in horizontal strokes. Blood gushed out through her dress and onto the floor.

She screamed again a weaker scream before she fainted.

The doctors and nurses ran to her aid and carried her out on a stretcher.

Nadia couldn't believe the nightmare she'd witnessed, worse than anything she thought possible and it scared her into a terrifying state of dread and misery.

They approached the medical room where a female doctor began patching her up as if it was another normal night at the clinic.

"What happened to that poor woman?" Nadia asked her, not expecting a detailed reply.

"She had an experimental drug today. We expected a little psychosis, because it's new to her, but we didn't expect it would make her psychotic, we need to adjust the dose because it's going to help cure her."

"When are you so-called experts going to learn that you can't give a pill with shock treatment and expect sanity after the trauma you've put her through?"

The doctor smiled. "Everyone leaves here sane, you will too."

The wound in my arm hurts but nothing compares to what Aisha has done to herself. These criminals will stop at nothing until they achieve what they're paid for.

Whatever that drug was really made her a monster. A skinny whippet with that kind of strength, how can a pill do that?

*If I don't get out of here fast, they'll carry **me** out on a stretcher covered in blood.*

* * *

Hidden Evil

The next morning after the nurse changed Nadia's bandages and gave her pain relief, she went to the restaurant with the other patients, feeling frightened of all of them as she reflected on what she'd seen the previous night.

The pain of her wound became bearable once the new pain medication kicked in, but her mind was playing tricks on her. She sat alone in silence and drank coffee but couldn't stomach breakfast. She felt helpless.

* * *

Afterwards a nurse escorted her to the therapy room where she lay down again on the same white leather chaise longue, feeling anxious while awaiting her next indoctrination therapy session.

Doctor Hancock arrived and made notes after sitting on the matching chair facing her.

"How are you feeling after the unfortunate incident yesterday?" he asked as he pushed his glasses towards his eyes, stopping them from falling off the end of his nose.

"I'm devastated for Aisha. Seeing her like that shows her treatment isn't working. I'm glad mine is because I want to go home and get on with my life," Nadia replied in a daze.

"Well, only you can make that happen once you've conformed to the program. I need to ask you the same questions again today and hope to receive different answers."

"I'm ready."

"When you leave here will you get divorced and never see Grace again?"

"Yes."

He slowly stood and walked across the room. "Would you like a glass of water?" he asked her.

"No thanks."

"Do you know how long you've been here, Nadia?"

"Days, weeks, months... it must be months."

"Do you know why you're here?"

"To punish me."

"No, we bring women here to cure them, to make them sane. Nobody ever leaves here uncured."

"Why don't you let me go now I'm cured?"

"We need to be absolutely certain that the flaw you acquired from western values, and the stain you've put on your society, has been wiped out. That you understand what we've done to you and it must be from your own free will to comply.

"We don't want to punish you we want to convert you. To completely capture your inner mind, leaving it reshaped after we've burned all evil out of you.

"We'll bring not merely an appearance of confession of evil but a genuinely heart-and-soul realisation of your flaw. We must make you one of us in our normalised society before your exit. No one ever stands out against us here, our treatment program is the best on earth. I can see it's working well for you. I have led you step by step to which there is no return to your old lifestyle.

"Never again will you be capable of love with another woman, or experience any joy out of the filth that you had previously. We have squeezed you empty and filled you with normality so your soul will cleanse and be forgiven on judgement day. You have controlled your own mind since you arrived and now you are ready to love a man and marry him."

Nadia spoke softly with determination. "I understand and agree. I'm ready to go home now."

"Over these past weeks, you have disagreed with me and deliberately tried to persuade me that you're telling the truth when I knew you were lying, but now you see how the mind can be controlled and washed clean. How I have broken you down so you have learned to control your mind, to accept humility and to control your will to rehabilitate your own mind."

"Yes, I have. I'm ready. I'm cured."

"Stand up, Nadia, come with me." He guided her towards a cupboard and opened it, exposing a long mirror.

"It's been a long time since you've seen yourself, Nadia, look." He moved away as she approached it and stared at the woman in the mirror.

It wasn't her anymore, she'd gone, she had betrayed Grace. She was a new woman beaten into submission.

What have they done to me? Who am I?

"You have endured degradation here and come out the other end a new shining example of our treatment, you're a better woman than the one I first met. Now you are sane and almost ready to leave here."

She walked towards him and grabbed him, throwing herself into his arms, crying helplessly.

"You will be released soon."

He reciprocated, holding her close with a smirk of successful recognition.

Chapter Twenty

Captain Lincoln arrived back to Dubai Offshore port with precision. Jenny and Grace helped pull down the sails and set out the fenders ready to dock in berth thirty.

"Welcome back to the sandpit," Jenny said.

"I don't know how to thank you both for saving my son and getting him out. You're my heroes now and forever."

"It was our pleasure." Jenny gave Grace a firm hug.

"All the best with your search for Nadia. You take care of yourself." Lincoln shook Grace's hand then pulled her in for an embrace.

Jenny embraced her again then they waved goodbye.

Grace stepped off the deck and walked towards the entrance passing the bustling restaurant with loud music, to find a taxi outside on the busy road.

The sun was blazing, she wiped away the trickles of sweat swept across her top lip with her fingers. Then stood inside an air-conditioned bus shelter to cool off and flag down a taxi. Sitting inside the cool shelter she felt safe to call Rita using her new sim card.

"Hi Rita, this is my new number. Darcy's safe with my parents."

"Hi Grace, well done. It's good to hear your voice and know you're back safe. I have good news for you. We've found the clinic in the desert and I have the perfect man to take you there and help you get Nadia out. Come to the safehouse and I'll arrange a meeting."

"Thanks so much, that's such a relief. I'm on my way once I get a taxi. See you soon."

Grace hailed the next available taxi that drove her along the Jumeirah Beach Road, passing the large villas of various old and contemporary styles. Most of the villas were already converted into business premises. Dentists, doctors, cosmetic surgeons, beauty salons, restaurants, cafés and spas adorned the road.

The taxi stopped at the safehouse.

Once inside the villa, she called her parents to stop them from worrying and spoke to Darcy.

As she showered the sea salt from her hair and body, she felt a little more relieved for the first time since that Friday morning when she was arrested.

She quickly dried off and dressed to answer the front door. A tall broad-shouldered man stood wearing a big friendly smile, a white t-shirt and black shorts and trainers. He was sweating intensely in the heat, looking like he had jogged all the way to the villa.

"Hello. Grace Peters?" he asked in a Nigerian accent.

"Yes, and you are?"

"I'm Kenneth. Rita sent me to meet you to discuss the plan to rescue your wife."

Grace held out her hand to shake his. "Come in, would you like a drink?"

"A cold beer please. Phew it's boiling out there." He wiped his forehead, face and neck with a flannel from his pocket.

Grace rummaged through the fridge to find beers and handed one to him as she opened one for herself. She gestured for him to follow her into the living room and they sat on a red sofa sipping cool beers in the chilled air-conditioning.

"I hear you've had it pretty tough since you arrived in Dubai," Kenneth said.

"Tough doesn't explain the depth of what we've all been through. I've been deliberately arrested to get me out of the way, whilst a vicious privileged family of elitist Emiratis play with our lives. I'm desperate to get my wife safely home to London."

"Well, Grace, that's where I come in. I can help get you both out of here on a private jet and safely home." He smiled confidently as he sipped his chilled beer.

Grace thought him a little *too* confident. "What qualifies you to help me, if you don't mind me asking?"

"I'm an experienced minder. I take care of security for one of the princesses here. She's eight months pregnant now and has been medically advised to stay in bed and rest in hospital under supervision until the baby is born. So, I am free to help a client of Rita's. I have dealt with various complicated situations like this over the years, both here in the Emirates and over in Saudi Arabia. You can trust me. I'll do my very best to help you."

"I always trust people I meet until they prove me wrong, but recent events have left me with less desire to trust anyone again except Rita and her team of experts, like you. I'd be lost without her knowledge. I still can't believe they're getting away with what they've done to Nadia." Grace put her head in her hands in despair as she thought of the nightmare Nadia would be facing.

"We have a helicopter ready to leave at 07.30 tomorrow. It will take us to the clinic. Wear the full abaya, you must pose as her visiting cousin. You will need both your passports, so we can get you across the border legally. The best way out of here is on a private jet but they'll check your passports on the plane just before departure. I'll collect you at 07.00." He stood to leave.

"Is there anything else I need to know? It seems too easy."

"Let's hope it goes smoothly, the jet will be ready to fly you both out safely, see you tomorrow and thanks for the beer." He smiled as he drank the last drop and handed the can back to her.

She walked him to the door and thanked him as she shook his hand again.

The villa was quiet.

Hidden Evil

She had the urge to drink more beer, so opened another one, drank it and went to her room to nap.

Feeling exhausted from the night watch at sea the previous night and the whole situation, her body ached for rest and her eyes were heavy.

After setting her alarm, she tossed and turned until she finally slept.

Chapter Twenty-One

Grace woke early without her alarm. She lay silent as she listened to the early birdsong, feeling refreshed from her rest but anxious about the day ahead. She wanted Nadia safe in her arms, far away from her corrupt family.

Grace showered and dressed in t-shirt and shorts, knowing how hot she would get under the abaya in a thirty-eight-degree heatwave. She moved into the kitchen and made herself breakfast of toast with jam from a pinewood cupboard. The coffee was hot and bitter but she told herself she needed it to stay alert.

As she sat at the counter with matching chairs, eating slowly to allow the food to go down, she felt her hands tremble slightly. She knew today would be tough and dangerous for them all; breaking out Nadia wouldn't be easy but she trusted Kenneth. He seemed like a man who knew how to do anything he put his mind to.

Grace packed a few of her belongings from her

suitcase and placed them into her backpack along with their passports and her untraceable phone. She paid no attention to what she might want or need to take and discarded the suitcase full of the rest of her new holiday clothes that she hadn't had chance to wear.

At 07.00 Kenneth drove into the driveway and honked his horn once. She stepped outside into the blazing hot morning, wearing full black abaya and black shades, carrying the small backpack. She waved to acknowledge him as she walked up the driveway and sat next to him in his white jeep.

"Good morning," he said with another huge smile.

"You seem happy and carefree. I wish I did."

"No point me worrying you. I can see how nervous you are but you shouldn't be. Everything is set and things will go to plan. I'm confident that I have the right people in place, ready to help. In a few hours your nightmares will be over."

He drove them along the Jumeirah Beach Road passing vibrant cafes bustling with people of all nationalities, waiters busily serving breakfast and coffees. The road's three lanes each side, lined with palm trees on both sides, were packed with vehicles in a rush to get to their destinations.

The music played loudly in some cars but quieter in Kenneth's jeep. He wasn't looking to draw attention to themselves as he slipped onto the junction towards the cargo side of the airport.

He parked up and led her to the helicopter where the pilot waited with his engine running. She stepped inside and smelt the newness of the leather interior.

Hidden Evil

She'd never been in a helicopter and the dials seemed immensely confusing upon first sight, it made her slightly nervous, adding to the tension inside her gut.

Kenneth climbed in afterwards and introduced them. "Hi Steve, this is Grace."

"Nice to meet you, Grace," Steve said in a Southern Australian accent, as he shook her hand.

"Same here. I wish it was under different circumstances but thank you for helping us out."

"It's my pleasure to be of assistance. Buckle up, put on the headphones, we're going up now." He winked then pushed and pulled switches, preparing to ascend.

They buckled in their seatbelts and placed the headsets on as the helicopter ascended into the bright sky. Grace noticed the tinted dark glass, done to keep the sun out and felt the freezing air-conditioning on her face and hands as the hatch slid shut.

Her stomach filled with butterflies. She was both excited and anxious at the speed of acceleration across the skyline of the city.

She looked down onto a glorious spectacle of skyscrapers, each with its own height, design and colour. The morning sun lit up their sides, giving an array of sunlight and shade bouncing off the glassed structures. The roads below looked like long worms and the swimming pools became the size of matchboxes, blue and inviting. For a few seconds she forgot why she was in it, she enjoyed the exhilarating experience without distraction from her overbearing anxiety.

Then the city was behind them in the distance.

Below she saw only sand in the barren desert blowing in the slight wind.

"Drinks are in the cooler, help yourselves and pass me a water please," Steve instructed.

Kenneth opened the cooler and passed a small bottle of water to him, took one for himself and offered one to Grace. They sipped in silence for few moments before Steve gave instructions.

"When we arrive, I will land on their helipad next to the building. I will stay inside and cut the engine. You two will go directly to reception and ask to visit Nadia. Family have been allowed. This confirms to me that she must be calmer now, by either accepting that she needs be to get visitors until she gets out of there, or the treatments have actually worked on her."

"What do you mean, the treatments have worked on her?" Grace asked.

"From my experience with the patients here some act falsely by making the psychologists believe they've changed or they do actually change completely. We can't tell anything until you see her and confirm for yourself, but that doesn't make any difference to our mission. We'll still be getting her out either way."

Given the pain on Grace's face upon realisation that Nadia would no longer be the woman she knew and loved, Kenneth put his arm around her to comfort her.

"Try not to be too concerned. It depends on how strong she is. I'm sure she'll recognise you and all will be fine."

Grace sat still and dazed into the desert, knowing

that the next few minutes would define the next chapter of their lives. She didn't want to imagine the worst, that Nadia won't remember her or their life together. Feelings of certainty arose, she knew that strong-willed Nadia would be faking whatever she needed to, and fighting to retain her sanity, doing anything to get out, as the sane Nadia imprisoned weeks earlier.

Steve landed on the helipad and cut the engine next to the large white building full of small windows and a protruding entrance. Grace and Kenneth walked slowly to the entrance and into the cold clinical reception, where the receptionist sat reading a magazine and only looked up when they approached the desk.

"May I help you?" she asked.

"We're here to visit Nadia Aktoum, I'm her cousin and he is my bodyguard," Grace told her in broken English attempting to sound Arabic but failed, thankfully going unnoticed by the receptionist.

"He must wait there, only women are allowed to visit women." The receptionist pointed at the sofa for Kenneth to wait.

"Okay, where is she?" Grace asked.

"Follow me, she's in the day room reading the Quran."

Grace remained calm, knowing that Nadia always enjoyed reading it quietly to herself and often out loud to her and Darcy.

Chapter Twenty-Two

As they entered the blue smooth-walled day room covered in a white tiled floor with yellow velvet chairs and white side tables, Grace noticed Nadia immediately, sitting in the corner reading the Quran. She didn't look up as they approached her.

"Miss Aktoum, your cousin has come to visit you," a nurse said as she moved a chair closer for Grace to sit on to face Nadia.

Nadia looked up and smiled but something was missing. "Hi."

The sparkle in her big black eyes had gone. They were soulless. Grace decided not to ponder on it, believing that Nadia was faking in front of the other patients, staff and CCTV cameras.

"Hi Nadia, how are you feeling?" Grace asked, waiting for the nurse to leave them alone.

"I feel better for seeing a smiling face. I can't stand it in here. I want to leave and as soon as I've finished the Quran, I'll go home to my parents."

Grace sat on the chair facing her as the nurse disappeared to fetch drinks for them. Grace became overwhelmed as a shudder passed down her spine, she bit her lip to stop her tears and knelt down beside Nadia to hold her, she didn't want this moment to end. It seemed a lifetime since she'd held her and felt her soft hair on her face and the warmth of her breath.

"I've come to take you home to London with me and Darcy, who's missing you so much. He's safe with my parents, waiting for us both. We're leaving, come with me," Grace whispered as she stood and gently held her arm to go outside.

"I can't leave until I've read the Quran and able to quote verses from it to the psychologist. He told me that's the only way I can leave here."

"Don't be silly, you can leave now with me, no one is going to rule our lives. There's a helicopter waiting for us, we must be quick, come on." Grace grabbed her arm with force as if to wake her from oblivion.

Nadia pulled away, sank back into her chair, and placed the Quran on the side table after slowly putting the binder into the page that she was reading. She folded her arms and looked around the room.

"What are you waiting for? We need to move quickly before the nurse comes back!" Grace insisted.

"Who are you to tell me to go against what my psychologist has told me to do?"

"Nadia, it's me, Grace, your wife!"

"I'm certainly not married and definitely not to you."

Hidden Evil

* * *

Kenneth arrived at the door and poked his head inside to find out what the delay was. He noticed Grace kneeling at the chair where Nadia sat. She looked over to him and summoned him towards them with pleading eyes.

He moved swiftly into the room after checking that the nurse was nowhere in sight.

"Come on, we must go now!" he whispered to them.

"Who are you?" Nadia asked.

"He's here to help me rescue you and take you home to London," Grace said.

"I'm not going anywhere with him. I'm waiting for my parents to come and collect me, once I've memorised the Quran," Nadia said again more softly, looking away from them.

* * *

"What have they done to you?" Grace said in disbelief, biting her lip to control her anger.

"We need to move now, Grace, come on," Kenneth insisted. "Help me to get her up and into the helicopter."

They grabbed one arm each and dragged Nadia out of the room screaming. The noise alerted the nurse and two security men arrived into the corridor to stop them.

"Get out of here before I call the police!" a guard shouted.

"Call the police, go on. I'm not leaving without my wife!" Grace shouted, knowing they would not call the police to come to an unregistered illegal prison facility.

The guards reached for their guns and pointed them towards Kenneth and Grace. Both too shocked to speak and scared to take action, they had no choice but to leave without Nadia.

"We'll be back for you, Nadia, as soon as we can." Grace embraced Nadia again and held her tightly. Nadia offered no response but pushed away and walked back into the day room to read the Quran.

"There's no way you're getting back in here. We know who you are and you won't be allowed in next time," the receptionist said with a red angry face as they passed by.

Outside Grace trembled with confusion, frustration and failure. She hadn't quite digested what she had witnessed, inside that cold clinic and an even-colder Nadia. Then the tears came.

Kenneth guided her back to the helicopter where Steve waited patiently. He started up the engine as they sat inside.

"Where is she?" Steve asked.

Kenneth answered. "She's not coming with us today."

"Will she ever?" Grace said under her tears.

"This has happened before. Her treatments must have been severe. We can try again next week," Steve replied, looking towards Kenneth for acknowledgement.

The helicopter moved towards the blue sky as Kenneth buckled himself and Grace into the belts and placed on headsets.

Grace sat without movement or words as she looked back at the clinic in the distance.

The sand dust hurled around them, and the clinic finally disappeared.

Chapter Twenty-Three

The helicopter landed at the cargo side of the airport and they both exited to return to Kenneth's car.

"Thanks Steve, I'll be in touch soon," Kenneth told him as they shook hands.

Grace paid no attention to their conversation. She removed her belt and headset and walked with her head down towards the car, where she remained silent as she pulled off the abaya and threw it on the back seat. Her breath was heavy, as Kenneth drove back towards the safehouse.

Grace broke the silence. "I need a drink, where can we get one now?"

"It's only nine thirty, are you sure?"

"I'm sure."

"I'll call Captain Lincoln, he always has booze on the boat and it's safe to drink offshore at this early hour, in case we're being monitored by the military. I'll ask him to get us back on the guest list to enter." Kenneth called Lincoln and drove to the sailing club.

Once through the security he parked in the guest parking and they walked along the boardwalk passed the bustling restaurant to the boat, where they were greeted by Jenny.

"Welcome aboard, guys. Lincoln's gone for refreshments at the clubhouse. He'll be back soon."

Grace was in tears so Jenny reached out to embrace her.

They settled on the front deck as Jenny poured a gin and tonic for Grace and offered a cold beer to Kenneth. "Here, Grace, get that down you. Tell me what happened."

"Thanks Jenny. I don't know where to start. I'm still in shock, this all seems so surreal."

Kenneth explained. "Nadia didn't seem to remember that she's married to Grace and refused to leave the clinic until she's able to memorise the Quran."

"Do you think she's faking memory loss or have their techniques worked?" Jenny asked.

Grace shrugged. "I've known her for nine years but I can't tell what she's doing. She seemed to recognise my face and smiled at me, but it was a look you'd give someone you haven't seen for years and she told me she's not married and definitely not to me. She was adamant that she didn't want to leave. If she's faking it, why didn't she just walk out with me? She could have easily got out." Grace swallowed a gulp of her drink and wiped her watery eyes.

"She could be faking it, knowing that there's CCTV cameras everywhere and not wanting to cause herself or you any harm, maybe," Kenneth added weakly.

"I've seen documentaries about these conversion therapy places in the USA, they're unsuccessful, but some of the young adults fake it for their parents, just to get out safely," Jenny reminded them.

"It's those same parents that pretend to cry on camera after they hear what hell their kids have been put through, in the name of written religion and negative shame of what their communities think. When they knew all along exactly what goes on inside these quack centres and they pay large amounts of dollars to get their kids into them for so-called conversion therapy."

Lincoln arrived aboard with drinks and hot breakfast sandwiches. He offered Grace one first, but she refused. "What's plan B?" Lincoln asked when the situation had been explained to him.

"Steve suggested going back next week," Kenneth added.

Grace shook her head. "That's too long... I need to get her out of there before they do more damage. She's unrecognisable. I don't know how to save her. I feel useless." Grace whimpered through tears of frustration. She stood, moving her chair and turning her back from the table.

Looking out across the windy ocean, she felt the water spray across her face. Then tears came again.

Lincoln scratched his grey beard when Grace finally turned back to the group. "You've saved Darcy from that vicious corrupt family, be proud of yourself. We need to find a way to speak to Nadia on her own."

Chapter Twenty-Four

Fatima woke early, excited to prepare for Nadia's return home from the clinic and become part of their family again.

I've been waiting for this moment for a long time. Ever since I discovered that scheming Grace wasn't Nadia's best friend after all. How dare they upset my family and defy Allah. How dare they insist on staying in that sinful society and raising my grandson to grow up without morals or ethics.

I can't stand the idea of my flesh and blood being brainwashed by Lucifer's deceit, living in criminality, accepting pornography and sexual exploitation as normal. Educating their children in gender ideology and mutilating them in order to further destroy themselves, all for profit by the criminals in charge.

A society that has been indoctrinated into not caring about being civilised and taking care of their children anymore. They fool themselves into believing they're liberated, when their traditional culture is being destroyed from the inside. A society who've tragically been sold not to believe in Heaven or Hell or Judgement Day when it arrives. Being promoted in the guise of diversity, independence, inclusion and fun to do what they want. Ignoring our creator and the glory bestowed upon us.

Grace will go back to where she belongs, Nadia and Darcy have been saved. She'll marry her cousin, who has taken a wife who cannot give him a child. He's ready for his second wife and that will be my Nadia. Just like I had planned when they were small children. They've always been a match made in heaven.

Everything will be perfect now Nadia has seen sense and is ready to be a Nassir's wife. She's going to look beautiful in her bridal gown, with bridesmaids and page boys to set the scene of a blissful lifelong perfect marriage.

"What time will you be ready to leave, habib?" Fatima lovingly asked Mohammad as she sat at her dressing table finishing off her make-up.

He smiled at her exuberance. "09.00, you have reminded me a dozen times."

"I don't want to be late but we must miss the rush-hour traffic, you know I hate to sit in it."

"I'll be ready, let's have breakfast in peace."

They moved down the two-metre wide swirling staircase of marble steps, with cast-iron railings, down to a long corridor of their eight-bedroom mansion, into the kitchen, where the cooks were preparing breakfast for the two of them.

The dining room table set for two looked sparse as

the other twelve yellow-gold velvet chairs sat empty. They made themselves comfortable as the uniformed maids, wearing white with matching hijabs, poured orange juice into their glasses and left the teapot for Fatima to pour when she was ready.

Two further maids proceeded into the dining room with the rest of the food laid upon silver platters, covered over to maintain heat. They placed them down in the centre of the table. "Will that will be all, madam?"

"Thank you," Fatima and Mohammad echoed to the maids as they left the room in a neat line.

"Any news on the whereabouts of Grace and Darcy?" Fatima asked her husband as he tucked into his eggs and bread.

"No idea but they haven't left Dubai. She's removed her sim card so we can't track her anymore. I have all airports, land and ports alerted, so I'll know immediately when they try to leave and get Darcy back with us."

"I'd hoped they'd gone by now. I don't want her to be in touch with Nadia again, especially after yesterday's commotion at the clinic. Nadia was severely upset and couldn't sleep last night. She called me twice asking why this woman from her past wanted her to go to London."

"I'm still surprised that the treatment has worked on her. She was a stubborn kid and has been since I can remember, strong-willed like her brothers. It must be worth the money they've charged us, if the treatment is working on her."

"I told you it transformed Zeina, Ali's daughter, although she was younger when she visited a clinic abroad. This new clinic is developing a reputation amongst the elite, for controlling unruly young women and girls, those who want to go against religion and become westernised, which is terrible for our families and for the future of our culture."

They finished breakfast and headed to the door as the maids marched in to clean up afterwards. Another maid swiftly opened the large wooden front door, to allow them to pass through it.

"Make sure everything is perfect for my daughter's return," Fatima reminded the maid.

The maid nodded.

Fatima and Mohammad drove along the main roads to the airport where the helicopter awaited. Once they'd strapped in and placed their headsets, they drank water and arrived soon after at the clinic. It was Fatima's fourth visit but Mohammad's second flight there. Men were not allowed to visit but can drop and collect their women.

They walked anxiously into the day room where Nadia sat waiting for them. She was wearing new clothes Fatima had purchased on a shopping trip with Jamila; a white smart designer blouse with smart black trousers with matching designer loafer shoes.

"Hello darling, don't you look smart today," Fatima said as she embraced Nadia.

"Hi Mother. Father, it's good to see you after all this time." Nadia stared at him.

"I saw you a few weeks ago." He looked puzzled towards Fatima.

"Time flies when you've been unwell, you're better now," Fatima said quickly to dismiss their conversation.

* * *

The nurse attempted to put Nadia's Quran into her bag but Nadia insisted it should stay with her to keep learning it off by heart. She knew instinctively this had become crucial to her full recovery after her mental illness.

The gentle nurse from Cape Town walked them to the exit door and said her goodbyes. As Nadia looked up at the blazing sun, her eyes closed. She searched her bag for her shades and put them on, following her parents to the helicopter to go to her home in Emirates Hills.

The helicopter lifted into the blue skies and returned to the airport, where their car was waiting to take them the rest of the journey.

As Nadia stepped out of the helicopter, she thought she had a memory of getting in it the first time. She stood still and looked around, as if to remember it, but the memory soon disappeared. It must have been a dream.

They arrived home to the beautiful mansion, where the maids greeted her with smiles. She thought she recognised one of them but she knew she had not met them before. The mansion seemed strange and she couldn't remember being there previously.

"We've put the sun loungers out by the pool for you to relax and wait for your sister to arrive and take a swim with you. I'm sure you both have a lot to catch up on." Fatima smiled with satisfaction.

Nadia agreed. "We've a *lot* to catch up on, I haven't seen Jamila for a long time, be nice to see her."

Mohammed looked at Fatima puzzled, he knew Jamila had visited with Fatima only the previous week to see Nadia in the clinic but dismissed his concerns and went off to change his clothes for work. He had far more important duties to concern himself with. Money laundering being his top priority.

Nadia went to her bedroom and changed into her bathing suit, then outside to read the Quran on the sun lounger, surrounded by luxury towels and white bath robes.

Water and soft drinks were put neatly on the side table in ice buckets. She lay down and gazed up at the bright sky. Feeling relaxed and glad to be home, away from Doctor Hancock and the machine that had made her better.

Chapter Twenty-Five

Jamila dropped her kids off at school and drove straight to Emirates Hills. When she arrived, she changed into her bathing suit and joined Nadia and her mother on the terrace by the poolside.

"Hi, how are you feeling today, sis?" Jamila asked Nadia nervously.

"I feel better thanks. I'm so happy to see you and be home again." She stood and embraced Jamila for longer than usual. Making Jamila feel edgy. She had only seen her the previous week but was acting like she had not seen her in years.

"Do you want sparkling or still water, Nadia?" Jamila asked as she walked to the tray of cold drinks and fruit.

"Still water please."

Jamila passed the water over and noticed Nadia looking down inspecting her stretchmarks around her own belly.

"The wonders of childbirth, I have more scars than you." Jamila pointed at hers and smiling.

"Did I have a baby?" Nadia asked.

"You have a son, Darcy, he's five now," Jamila said after hesitating to divulge the information. Not knowing how to continue their line of conversation or how to avoid her questions.

"I've been very ill, haven't I? I don't remember having a baby. Where is he?" Nadia held her head down and clutched the glass of water.

"He was with me but Grace took him and we can't find him. We don't know where they are." Jamila informed her as their mother joined them at the pool to offer her explanations.

"Your father and his colleagues will find little Darcy. Don't worry, love, he can't be far away. He'll be back with us soon, I assure you," Fatima said, as she rubbed sun lotion on Nadia's shoulders.

One of the maids arrived to enquire whether they wanted lunch at the pool or indoors.

"I'd like to eat outside please," Nadia said. "I haven't eaten outside for so long."

The others agreed it was the best solution even though it was reaching forty-two degrees.

"Who is Grace?" Nadia asked.

Jamila and Fatima stared at each other, ready to give their rehearsed answer.

"She's an old friend from Oxford University, remember, you studied Law together before you graduated," Fatima replied, smearing sun lotion on herself.

"I can't remember much of our friendship, it's all a blur. Were we *best* friends?"

"Not really," Fatima said as Jamila quickly moved to the edge of the pool and dived in to avoid speaking about Grace and lying to her big sister.

Fatima followed Jamila into the pool and they swam to the other side, leaving Nadia lying on the sun lounger alone.

"How can you continue to lie to her? I can't do it, it's disrespectful and absolutely wicked," Jamila whispered feeling deceitful holding back her tears.

"It's not wicked or disrespectful, don't you worry about it. Soon she won't ask us about Grace at all, but we must lie to her for now. It's for her own good, you know that. Then we can all get on with our lives," Fatima whispered.

"I hope this doesn't backfire on you, if she comes round and finds out what you've done, she'll never forgive you or Father. I can't be part of this, I won't help you ruin my sister's life. I'm leaving after lunch and I won't be back here for a while. I can't agree with what you've both done to her," Jamila blurted out.

"For the sake of Allah shut up, will you. We need to act normal in front of her." Fatima swam back to the sun loungers and wiped herself dry, smiling to Nadia as she lay down before sipping her chilled sparkling water.

Lunch was served on the balcony, outside the day room, overlooking the pool. The maids placed a white cloth on the outdoor dining table and laid it with silverware, white porcelain china and crystal glassware.

Large blue and white striped cushions sat on each chair to provide extra comfort. The electric water spraying fans had been set on highspeed cold.

    Jamila sat silent as she played with the food on her plate, unable to eat it. Nadia ate small mouthfuls and chewed slowly as Fatima scoffed her delicious lunch of fillet steak and assorted salad.

Chapter Twenty-Six

Grace woke with a banging headache from a gin and tonic hangover. Feeling sick, she went to the bathroom. As the shower water poured over her face, she slid down onto the floor inside the cubicle and wept. She had no idea how she was going to save Nadia and rescue her from her vicious controlling parents.

Then, after what seemed like hours of tears, she heard her phone ringing. She slipped on a towel and answered it.

"Hi Grace, how are you feeling?" It was Rita.

"Useless." Grace held her breath to stop hiccups caused by her latest outburst then swallowed the lump in her throat to speak more freely.

Rita continued. "I've just called the clinic, who told me that Nadia was signed out yesterday by her parents. I think they've taken her home but you need to speak to Jamila to find out."

"That's good news. Okay, I'll call her now, but what's the plan? I can't go to Emirates Hills. I'll have to ask Jamila if she can arrange a secret meeting for us, but I'm not sure how involved she's become in the deceit. She might be angry with me for taking Darcy off her."

"Call her and find out how she feels and if she'll help you to meet Nadia away from her parents' home, somewhere quiet, like the women-only spa on Emirates Road, near the hospital, not far from you. She can only say no if she's not ready to get involved, but it's worth a try isn't it?"

"Anything's worth trying. I'll call you back. Thanks again for all your help."

Grace dried herself off and dressed in a pale blue sleeveless cotton dress, before walking into the kitchen to make a strong sugary coffee with milk. The safehouse remained quiet as she took a few sips of hot coffee and went back to her bedroom.

She pondered and sat on the bed, before reaching for her original sim card packet and changed it back into the phone. Jamila would know it was her from the number.

Grace noticed her trembling hands as she searched for the number in her phone and wasn't sure if it was a combination of dehydration from alcohol or nervousness to the outcome of the conversation to be had with Jamila.

"Hi Jamila," Grace said as she heard Jamila breathing but not speaking. "Jamila, is that you?"

"Yes, it's me."

"I hear Nadia's left the clinic, is that true?"

"Yes, she came home yesterday with my parents."

"How is she?"

"She seems like a different person. She doesn't remember the last few years of her life. It's like it's been erased completely. She didn't even know she has a son." Jamila began to breathe heavier and then the tears came.

Grace was delighted that Jamila had answered the call and offered updates. She did all she could to hold her own tears, while attempting to comfort Jamila. She was close to meeting up with Nadia, she didn't want to ruin that chance.

"I understand how heartbreaking this is for you as much as me, but it must be brutally antagonising for Nadia. Imagine how she feels and what she must be going through in her tethered mind."

"I don't think she realises anything at all. She's completely lost. I don't know if that's a good thing for anyone but seeing her this way, is so wrong on every level. I can't believe the therapy worked so well on her. I didn't think it would. You know how strong-minded she can be."

"We both know how strong-willed she is. We have no idea how this treatment has affected her now or in the long term, or if she'll ever recover or be herself again."

"I can't think straight anymore, I can't sleep knowing what my parents have done and what they are capable of. It scares me out to know they have this type of power over us." Jamila continued to sob into the phone.

"Listen, Jamila, is there any way you can bring her for a day out at the Emirates women's spa, so I can see her again one last time before I go home back to London?"

"I don't know if that's possible, yesterday I told Mother that I can't be part of what they're doing and won't be going to see them again for a while. I can't face it all, it's too distressing."

"I'm happy to hear you're on Nadia's side and want the best for her, but imagine how distressed *she* is. Will you think about it please? You could say that you've changed your mind and want to get to know the new Nadia and spend time alone with her in a safe setting."

"Okay leave it with me. I'll do anything to see Nadia smile again. If it means going against my parents then so be it. They scare me but I'll think of how to organise a meeting and get back to you later."

"I can't thank you enough for your kindness, Jamila. I don't know what we'd both do without you. I know you love her as much as I do and want only the best for your big sister."

"Is Darcy safe? You don't need to tell me where he is but I need to know he's safe."

"There's no need to worry about him. He misses us but yes, he's safe."

"Good to know, I'll call you later. Bye for now."

"Thanks Jamila, bye."

Grace felt her belly rumble for food, a sign of reduced anxiety. She decided to go out and find a restaurant close by and prepare for the meeting with Nadia.

Grace walked along the busy street of international café' and restaurants, where she decided to eat

Lebanese food, to remind her of the days when she'd first met Nadia, who'd introduced her to the delicious Lebanese cuisine, at a restaurant in Oxford, and later when they had dined in a selection of Arabic restaurants on the Edgware Road, London.

The waiter greeted her and offered her a menu with a smile as she sat near the window inside, looking out onto the street. She felt the air-conditioning hit her body immediately after the heat outside. She noticed looking in the window that her hair had dried quickly in the sun and made her look like a typical tourist, without a care in the world. If only, she thought as she searched the menu for Filafil and Tabouli with Shish Tawook chicken skewers.

* * *

After she ordered, she took out her phone to make notes of what she would talk about to get Nadia to remember them being together. It wasn't difficult because they had so many wonderful memories to share.

1. How they'd met.
2. When they'd graduated.
3. When they'd both secured jobs in top law firms.
4. When they'd moved to London together.
5. When they'd got married.
6. When they'd sailed around the Islands of Thailand.
7. When they'd decided who should be pregnant.
8. When Darcy arrived.

9. When they went on happy holidays as a family. Before this one.

She found herself getting a lump in her throat as her hands trembled and stopped typing into her notes. Why was she anxious again? Was it their fabulous memories or the thought of not making new ones together? She wouldn't dare think about the latter and placed her phone on the table to eat the delights in front of her.

She paid in cash, so not to leave any trace of her bank card. Mohammad and his spies would be tracking her every move. He may already know that she called Jamila but Grace had had no choice but to use her original number, then she panicked and rushed into the toilet. Her phone was still on awaiting the call from Jamila to confirm the meeting.

Feeling useless under pressure, not sure what to do, Grace called Rita.

"Hi Rita , I spoke to Jamila using my old sim card from the safehouse and it's still in my phone at the restaurant, because I'm waiting for her to call me back and confirm. I'm not sure what to do now. I'm losing my mind and not thinking strategically anymore!"

"Don't worry, it's done now, best to stay where you are until you get the call and then switch the sim cards before you return home."

"Okay, I'll stay and have a drink to ease my hangover. Call you later once I know. Bye."

Grace sat back down at her table and ordered

Hidden Evil

another bottle of water and a coffee. Staring out of the window, watching the cars pass by seemed an eternity, but eventually the call arrived.

"Hi Jamila."

'Hi. I've told Mother I'm taking Nadia to the water park tomorrow for the day but we'll meet you at Emirates women's spa instead. See you at 10am, okay."

"Thanks so much. See you tomorrow."

Grace replaced her sim card and called Rita with updates.

"I'm going to bring Nadia with me to the safehouse tomorrow and then plan how to get her out of Dubai safely."

"That's a good plan, keep me updated. Bye for now."

As Grace walked outside, the humidity hit her but she didn't let that bother her. She had a new plan to organise and keep her focused.

* * *

Back at the safehouse she showered off the sweat from walking in the heat and changed into shorts and t-shirt, then drank a beer to calm her nerves and relax on the FaceTime call to update her parents and check on Darcy.

"You've called too early for Darcy, he's at school," Susan reminded her.

"I know but I wanted to update you on the situation here. I'll call back later to parent Darcy over FaceTime." Grace chuckled.

"FaceTime parenting is no joke, Grace. He misses you both and keeps asking me when you'll be home. How much longer will you be?"

"Hopefully we can fly out of here the day after tomorrow, once I've got Nadia away from them, it will be easier to arrange a safe exit home. I can't put anything in place until I have her here with me."

"I hope it goes well, darling, I really do. I'm worried about you both so much and the thought of you getting arrested again scares me."

"I'm worried too but what choice do I have? You know I can't just up and leave her here to be controlled by them."

"I know, I know, but I'm your mother and it's my job to worry about you."

"I'll call you later when Darcy's home from school, okay. Bye for now. Love you, Mom."

"Love you more, bye."

Chapter Twenty-Seven

Later that day, after Grace had spoken to Darcy, she sat alone in the living room, going over and over the things she'd say to enable Nadia to remember her life over the last few years. Feeling assured that nothing would get in their way, Grace lay down mentally exhausted on the couch for a nap.

She woke startled by the arrival of Kenneth and his loud friend Brian from Birmingham England. Kenneth had mentioned him previously and that he'd been working in Dubai for seven years with a multinational corporation, selling wealth investments to expatriates of all nations.

Kenneth introduced them. "Hi Grace, this is Brian. I had a call from Rita to bring him here from the police station in Bur Dubai. They've arrested him for bouncing a cheque on his landlord."

"Hi Brian, nice to meet you. Can I get you both a beer?" Grace asked as she stood up to shake hands.

"That'd be good thanks," they echoed.

Grace returned with three ice-cold beers, grateful for the distraction of her own living hell.

Brian explained his situation. "There's been some confusion. I gave my landlord notice to leave after my annual tenancy but he hadn't cashed my cheque last year. I didn't notice as I'm hopeless with accounting and since then I've changed my bank. So, when he tried to cash it, I was arrested for closing an account with outstanding balances. Once I realised it was a mistake, I wrote him a cheque from my new bank, which he cashed. I apologised and I thought that was it, over and done with, mistakes happen but I've still broken the law. I have no idea why he didn't cash my cheque for a year. My bank account has been frozen along with my credit cards. My passport is being held by the police until trial. I can't get my renewal work visa without my passport, which means I can't work anymore and to top it all off, I can't go home and visit family."

"I'm sure Rita will get you home," Grace said.

"I don't want to go home for good. I like it here, I'm earning a lot of money in my job without paying taxes. I can't get that back home. I've almost saved enough money to buy a house without a mortgage, that's why I came here, to save up. I want to stay and fight my corner because I'm innocent. I can easily pay a fine but there's a chance I'll go to prison for three years. I'm angry with myself for not being more assertive with my own banking. It just never occurred to me that anyone wouldn't cash a rent cheque for over twenty thousand pounds."

"That's the law here," Kenneth reminded him,

"and the sooner people realise that it's different to their laws the better it is for them. You're not alone, mate, so many innocent people get caught up without knowing that they're breaking laws."

"I hardly write cheques these days, most of my outgoings are online payments or I use my cards. I'm aware of most of the laws but not this one, I feel such a fool." Brian gulped his beer.

Grace felt somewhat relieved to know that she wasn't the only person in the safe house with legal problems. It helped take her mind off her own severe issues as they sat drinking beer, dissecting the differences in international law, something Grace was an expert on.

"Why are you here?" Brian asked Grace.

"I was falsely arrested when my wife went missing but she turned up after her parents abducted her to get her away from me. I'm awaiting my flight to go home."

"Blimey, that's a whole different ball game to my legal issues."

"Any chance of another beer?" Kenneth asked.

"In the fridge, you'll find crates of it. Get us all another one please." Grace winked to thank him as the conversation flowed about the difference in Sharia laws compared to constitutional western laws.

"Did you hear mainstream news reporting that a man ate a bagel with poppy seeds at Heathrow airport, got randomly searched and then arrested to take a urine sample, which showed he had opiates in his urine after consumption?" Brian asked them.

Kenneth nodded. "I heard that was made up to

highlight the dangers of bringing drugs into Dubai, so I'm not sure it's true."

"I heard he had more than poppy seeds but the sensational press love a good narrative." Grace said.

"I don't know what to believe these days, I know transporting across borders illegal narcotics is a global offence, but the law in Dubai is intolerant of some prescribed medications like codeine pain relief and that carries the standard four-year sentence." Brian told them.

"I heard about the foolish British man and his Syrian mate who attempted to sell three-fourths of an ounce of cannabis to an undercover copper here and both got a death sentence, but are still locked up. Nobody should be that stupid to sell to strangers anywhere it's still illegal," Grace told them.

"Those two fools will be locked up for a long time and keys to cells thrown away, they won't meet the firing squad like that paedophile monster did in 2017 for kidnapping, raping and murdering an eight-year-old boy. Although the man deserved the death penalty in my opinion," Kenneth said.

"What about the Lebanese man with his Russian girlfriend on holidays who drank orange juice at the gas station. A plain-clothed moral policeman arrested them for abusing Ramadan traditions by drinking in public.

"They were arrested and locked up to await trial. They were then fined only one thousand dirhams each but instantly deported upon release, ruining their holidays. Even I'm not that ignorant of Muslim traditions here. I know it's forbidden to drink or eat in public during the thirty days of sun hours fasting. Except in private hotels and homes if you're not Muslim," Brian said with a chuckle, forcing them all to join in the laughter.

"Aw come on, it's not fair to arrest tourists is it, they're blind to these customs and aren't aware that they're breaking the law. Just like you have, Brian," Grace said, feeling sorry for all of them.

"That's just it though, people blindly come on holiday and plead ignorance, but that doesn't wash here. They don't tolerate ignorance as a plea bargain excuse for intolerance to Sharia Laws. I have studied that case amongst others in the hope I only get a fine and not a custodial sentence or deportation. Rita will get me off like she did those two with only a fine, because they appointed her firm to help them at the trial," Brian concluded.

Grace raised her beer. "Let's drink to that."

They clinked bottles and slugged down the beer together.

Kenneth spoke next. "At least a few things have been changed for non-western foreigners working here now. Like confiscating passports and not paying proper wages to construction workers who lived in horrendous conditions and used as slave labour."

"How has it changed?" Grace asked, aware of the stories she had read in the British news.

"The government set up a secret helpline to call if you're being abused by your employers. They investigate and arrest these criminals and lock them up with long sentences, making it harder for these wasters in society to carry out these crimes against humanity," Kenneth told her.

"That's excellent news but what about the sex traffickers?" Grace asked.

"Sex trafficking is a global problem, not just here in Dubai. Young women can call the hotline number and be rescued, like in most countries, but many aren't aware of it and are always blackmailed into believing that their loved ones back home will be murdered if they attempt escape. Some women have no clue that this number exists and don't have access to a phone. It's the biggest crime towards humanity next to kidnapping," Kenneth said.

"God only knows what those women endure and he'll give them karma on judgement day." Grace felt uneasy at the thought of being enslaved into prostitution.

For a few hours that evening and the distractions of conversation, Grace felt her old self. She enjoyed discussing differing laws and criminals getting caught for crimes against humanity. Her feelings of helplessness towards Nadia vanished and then resurfaced continuously. Grace was feeling tired and drunk from the copious amounts of chilled beer.

"I'm beat and ready to sleep to be fresh in the morning," Grace said as she stood to go to bed.

Kenneth stood to say his goodbyes and shook Grace's hand. "Yeah, me too I should go now too. I have another rescue tomorrow."

"Oh no, I'm just getting started on the lash here,

you can't abandon a man to drink alone this early," Brian butted in.

They all laughed and wanted to stay to put the world to rights, but Kenneth's rescue operation was a life-and-death situation the next day and Grace was determined to rescue Nadia once and for all.

Later that night Grace lay awake in bed in the darkness, tossing and turning to try to find a comfortable position. She was mentally exhausted but couldn't sleep. Her mind was racing and covering all scenarios.

Eventually she dozed off, leaving Brian to lock up and retire.

Chapter Twenty-Eight

Grace stirred awake, still tired, to the sound of her alarm at 07.00. The house was quiet and she heard the birdsong outside as usual in the early morning. She sat up and drank water from the bottle on her bedside table.

She noticed that her hands no longer trembled but she still felt mentally exhausted and not ready for whatever the day would bring. The knot in her belly persisted.

In the kitchen she brewed coffee and made eggs on the previous day's bread, but couldn't eat anything, so she made more coffee to liven up.

I must get some food shopping in for Nadia later.

Grace showered and went to the bedroom to dress. She would usually have an outfit already planned out but she couldn't decide what to wear. She had nothing in her suitcase that Nadia would remember her ever wearing. All their clothes were new summer season that they had picked out together on an excited shopping trip, just after they had booked the flights to Dubai.

Grace packed her bikini in her backpack and sat on the bed wondering if it was worth packing anything else for the day at the spa. She decided to wear a loosely fitted linen dress. Nadia liked her to look feminine.

Grace smiled, remembering the day in the changing rooms in London. Those easy days when she felt elated at the idea of pleasing Nadia, not saving her from the pit of hell that Grace was now in.

It was still too early to call a taxi to the spa so she decided to tidy up their bedroom, she wanted it to look perfect when Nadia arrived later. She was an organised neat freak, always having everything in its place. 'Everything has its home,' Nadia always said.

* * *

Grace sat in the back of the taxi and noticed her hands began to tremble again. Nothing she could think of would stop them. She placed them on her lap and looked out at the busy roads with traffic everywhere, going in every direction.

When she arrived at the spa, she looked around the entrance but couldn't see them.

"Good morning. Have Nadia and Jamila gone in yet?" Grace asked the receptionist.

"You're the first here, no one has gone in yet. It's members only, do you have a guest invitation?"

"Yes, I'm waiting for my friends to arrive."

Hidden Evil

"Take a seat please, you need to be signed in."

She sat in the relaxed reception on a floral chair and smelled the Arabic incense wafting in the cool air-conditioning, that made her feel sick on an empty stomach.

She helped herself to another cup of water from the machine in the corner and gulped it down as members began to arrive at reception to sign in.

Women from all nations arrived smiling as they met up with family and friends, ready to enjoy a relaxing getaway at the spa. Some wearing full abaya and others dressed in casual attire. Then she saw them.

"Hi Nadia." Grace smiled nervously as Nadia entered the reception. Her hands still trembled awaiting acknowledgement.

"How are you, Grace?" Jamila asked as she kissed her on both cheeks.

"Hi Grace, I didn't expect to see you here!" Nadia replied with a genuinely warm smile.

They signed in at reception and went directly to the changing rooms, where they were greeted by a staff member offering them keys to lockers, towels, slippers and bath robes. Once they'd changed into their bikinis and placed on their towelled robe and slippers, they entered a large glassed balcony area and sat at a table.

"I'm going to the bathroom, order me the vegetable smoothie please," Jamila said as she looked at Grace and smiled as she walked away to leave them alone.

"It's me... do you remember me?" Grace asked as she turned to Nadia and squeezed her hands. Fear was etched onto her face as her words dropped like poison in her ears, awaiting the response.

"I know who you are, Grace," Nadia replied as she sat still and looked down at her lap, reciprocating Grace's grip.

"Why are you acting this way, like you don't know me at all? What do you remember about us?"

"I remember our friendship turned to profound love and we married and had an adorable son Darcy."

"Oh my god! That's fantastic! I thought they'd erased your memories completely. I've been devastated by what they've done to you, how they've treated you, telling you that your life isn't worth living with me, and your life isn't you own, and that you've been living against the wishes of god."

"I'm not surprised that my mother has lost respect for me or what she did to me. I needed that therapy to show me that I can be a normal daughter and make her proud of me again."

"What the hell is *that* supposed to mean?"

"I love you, Grace, but I must face reality and understand that my mother will never allow us to be happy together. She can't accept what I've done to the family, not marrying my second cousin as arranged and bringing shame to them. I have to put things right and stay here and start a new life. A life that she and Allah has prepared for me, one that she will be proud of."

"No! This isn't you. I can't accept this, Nadia. How can you so coldly say this? I love you, I will always love you and want you to come home with me. Darcy is waiting for us. You have a life in London and a career that needs you."

"My mother wants me to marry here and have more children with Nassir who has accepted me as his second wife. I have no choice but to go along with what they all want. I'm too tired to contest anymore, she's worn me out."

"That's ridiculous, of course you don't have to go along with any of this, why ever would you consider it? What's making you feel this way? You just said you loved me and you must remember how happy we are together. What's happened for you to change your mind?"

"I have this overwhelming feeling of being trapped. Like there's this big thing looming over me and I'm the only one who can see it. I have terrible daydreams and terrifying nightmares." Nadia squeezed her eyes closed and held onto Grace's hands.

"I think you need help with these new feelings of despair. It seems your therapy has done nothing but confuse your feelings of who you are. Do you feel like you have a future here with Nassir?"

"I can't seem to imagine any future for me at all. I feel like ending my life but I won't do that because that's the easy way out of all of this. Only a coward avoids pain, not me. I need the pain as it's the gateway to all of these changes. My therapist told me that many times. I have to endure the pain to recover and be normal again."

"I have never heard such bullshit from a therapist, this is total nonsense. You shouldn't be feeling like there's no future. Can you imagine your future without me and Darcy in it?"

Nadia stared coldly at Grace. "That's just it, I can't imagine any future with anyone!"

"Do you have those feelings of ending your life under control?"

"I can control them until I can't anymore. Isn't that the way it works?" Nadia swallowed, with fear in her eyes.

"So, you're saying you can't control these impulses?"

"No, I'm saying that it's a stupid question."

"Do you feel like hurting yourself, Nadia?"

"If I say yes, what will you do? How can you help me? Will you send me back to the therapist against my will, like my mother did?"

"No, never, but you're scaring me. I'm worried about you. This isn't you and you know it."

"I'm worried too. I remember holding Darcy when he was a baby, his small helpless body in my hands. The weight of him as I held this fragile thing and you get this jolt of fear because you know you could let him go and let him break on the floor. The possibility is right there, so close and you feel this dread, like there's some part of you that you can't control and you'll drop him, just to relieve you, just to make it go away. You know that feeling don't you, Grace."

"No, I don't know that feeling. It sounds like a crazy person's thoughts. Look, Nadia, you're not going to figure this out alone, let's go somewhere quiet and talk, just you and me alone together. Only I can help you get back to your old self, the person you love to be. The woman who can tackle anything that life throws at her. Come with me now, let's leave here." Grace stood and grabbed Nadia's arm out of sheer frustration.

"No! I'm not going anywhere with you. My mother was right, she told me you might to try to get me to go with you when I was in the clinic but I can't go with you. I'm staying here in Dubai with my family."

"We're your family too, Nadia. I love you and want to help you. Please come with me now and let's get some proper professional help together," Grace said as her tears poured.

"Did you order the drinks?" Jamila asked as she returned to the table. Seeing Grace in tears, she embraced her and called over the waitress to take their order to avoid unwanted attention in the café.

Jamila sat at the table and saw Nadia crying too. Her strong big sister was no longer the person she knew. She felt her own tears try to fall but stopped them. One of them needed to retain a sense of composure and decide on the next practical move.

"I'm not going to let you upset her, Grace. She's already a mess. I can't recognise her anymore. It's like being with a stranger, a ghost, with nothing in common. I've always looked up to her and admired her strength but not now. I need someone to believe in again and want it to be her but she's lost," Jamila whispered as she put her head down and held Nadia's hand.

"For God's sake, I don't want to upset her either but I can't stand by and watch what she's going through. I need to get her to come with me and get help. Can you tell her please?" Grace begged Jamila.

"Go where? You can't take her anywhere because my father will track you down and get her back. Her life has been planned out here before she went to Oxford and met you. Nadia's just going along now with what mother always wanted. Seems she wants to do it too. I don't understand either but she's willing to do what it takes to please Mother."

"It's a safehouse and he won't find us without tracking our sim cards. We'll take them out of our phones and we can stay there for a few days then get out of here for good once she sees sense. Will you help me please, Jamila?"

"How will you get her out of Dubai?"

"I have a way but it's best you don't know so don't ask me. I trust you, Jamila, I know you want the best for your big sister, just like I do."

The drinks arrived but they didn't touch them, no one felt the urge for sour vegetable smoothies in a busy café.

"Nadia, I want you to go with Grace to her place and stay for a while until you feel better and well enough to travel back to London," Jamila told Nadia.

"I'm not going anywhere with Grace it'll just cause her more trouble than she needs. I'm going home to Mother, where I belong, and Grace needs to go home safe to be with Darcy."

"Please Nadia come with me. I'm not leaving here

without you. You don't know what you're saying, you're all confused due to quack therapy and what it's done to you. It's made you believe that your mother knows what's best for you and that you must be loyal to her but you know she's never respected your wishes to live your own life, she's a bully who has concocted a vicious lie about dying of cancer just to get you here and turn you against me. Why can't you see her evil plan as it's unfolding?"

"Mother would never lie about such a thing, would she, Jamila?" Nadia turned towards her for confirmation.

"Actually, she had a cervical smear and they found white cells that had to be lasered out. That's all. It's not life threatening for Mother as they found them early and she's fine with regular annual checks, but you know how she is. She used her diagnosis to play on your heart strings and get you over here to enact her evil plan.

"She'd planned the whole thing for months without telling anyone the details. I wouldn't put it past her to lie about the laser treatment. She probably read it in a leaflet at the doctor's surgery, knowing her."

"That's not lying is it as it could've become cancerous and you can't confirm if she had the laser or not," Nadia replied.

Grace couldn't take any more. "Good god, it's not cancer is it though, Nadia. She lied again. She had me arrested the day they drugged you and took you to that clinic. They suggested that you'd been murdered by me as you'd disappeared.

"I spent two nights in a prison cell worried sick about you and whether you'd suffered an honour killing, lying dead buried in the desert. You must know that your mother is evil." Grace waved her hands in the air.

Nadia looked horrified. "I don't believe you. My father wouldn't go along with that."

"Grace is right, Nadia," Jamila explained. "They arrested her that same day and she spent the weekend locked up, not knowing where you were or if they'd harmed you in any way. She had to go to court and appeal her innocence."

"I was devastated, locked up in the dark by liars, not knowing what they'd done to you. I was petrified with fear not knowing where Darcy was. I've been in a living hell since that Friday morning. I need to get out of here and I'm not leaving without you Nadia," Grace said, with tears rolling down her cheeks.

"I can't believe what you're telling me. I'm so sorry for the way you've been treated. You don't deserve my mother doing those horrific things to you and that's why I have to stay here because none of us know what Mother is capable of next. She wants things her way and will stop at nothing to get it. She has my father's power alongside her vicious mind to hurt anyone and could make anyone disappear never to be seen again." Nadia was also sobbing uncontrollably.

"Your mother is evil but she isn't in London and she can't threaten you forever. Come with me. The safest place for you is far away from her. I've already risked a forty-year prison sentence to get Darcy out and will do anything to save us both," Grace said, frustrated, through teary eyes, not caring anymore if Jamila knew what she had done.

"Go with her Nadia and be safe in London," Jamila told her sister as she wiped her own tears with a napkin.

"I can't go anywhere but home to Mother because I fear for Grace and I don't want to put her in any more danger. She's better off without me and our vicious family. Go home, Grace, and take care of Darcy, he needs you more than ever because he can't see me again." Nadia continued sobbing.

Grace stood over her, enraged. "I can't believe what you're saying. Why are you accepting your fate here with that evil monster?"

"You don't understand and I can't explain it to anyone who isn't part of our family. Mother always gets her own way and if she doesn't then she'll make someone pay for it," Nadia told Grace.

"Please, Grace, go home to Darcy and I'll call you soon." Nadia stood and took Grace's arm to lift her off her chair she had just sat on and held her in a tight long embrace as if for the last time.

Grace couldn't let go.

They clung onto each other and sobbed. It was Jamila who eventually parted them as she pulled Nadia away and left Grace standing alone, trembling, after taking Nadia's new passport from her to keep safe.

Grace took a taxi and cried all the way back to the safehouse where she lay on the bed and cried more in rage at Fatima, frustration at her own lack of being her wife's saviour, and the helpless feeling that she'd lost Nadia forever.

Grace dozed off mentally exhausted and woke to the sound of her phone ringing. It was her mother.

"Hello darling. How's things? When are you both coming home?"

"I don't know. Nadia won't listen and insists I go home without her. She's staying to marry Nassir at the behest of her evil mother," Grace blurted out but couldn't believe her own words.

"Oh no. She sounds so screwed up. What's your plan now?"

"No idea yet. I'm running out of options." Grace held back sobs and swallowed the lump again in her throat.

In the car on the way back to Emirates Hills, Nadia cried silent tears of rage at her mother's dominating, cunning indoctrination, sadness at Grace's suffering by Nadia's horrific mother, and the feeling of complete loss of her own mind, sanity and identity.

Chapter Twenty-Nine

"Hello darlings, you're back early." Fatima smiled as her daughters walked into the sunlit day room.

"I said you're back early, didn't you hear me?" she sarcastically repeated.

"We heard you, Mother," Nadia replied with a vicious look towards her before she went upstairs to avoid any confrontation and to be alone after what Fatima had just subjected onto her loving wife.

"What's happened to Nadia?" Fatima asked Jamila, pointing at the door.

"What do you think happened? Surely you have a semblance of empathy making your daughter end her marriage to the woman she loves because of what you've done to her?" Jamila snapped as she swept her long dark hair off her face.

"She doesn't remember Grace or her life in London."

"That's what she's made you think but it's not true. She remembers everything, the treatment didn't work as you were sold it would. She's only going along with your plans because you've threatened to harm Grace if they get back together. She remembers it all, Mother, and she hates you with every bone in her body. Stop fooling yourself."

Fatima stood ready for confrontation. "I have done no such thing. How dare you suggest it."

"Just like you didn't try to drown my school friend Hassan in the pool or when you pushed Nadia's friend Zeina down the stairs to make them stay away from us!" Jamila shouted as she waved her arms in the air. She was standing behind the couch near to the door.

"They were accidents, you know they were." Fatima folded her arms in contempt and avoiding her own deceits and lies.

"Convenient accidents, more likely. You thought I was getting too close to Hassan and it would ruin your plans for my marriage to Mo. You knew back then that Nadia was a lesbian and her and Zeina were falling in love, didn't you? You've done everything you can to threaten our friends and ruin our lives, just to fulfil your own ideals of how we should live our lives." Jamila pointed towards the door, where Nadia had exited.

"I have no idea what you're implying but it's not true." Fatima sat on the couch and pulled up her sleeves.

"That's you all over; deny, deny everything you do

Hidden Evil

to get your own way. What would've been so wrong if I'd married Hassan? He's a respectable businessman from a good family. He loved me then and still does but you made it impossible for us to be together. I hate you for what you've done to me, and I hate you even more for what you're putting Nadia through . You are a monster.

Jamila grabbed a cushion from the couch and threw it at Fatima. "She was so happy with Grace and living in London with a fabulous career, and now you've killed all that. You're evil and Allah will punish you for it."

"How dare you speak to me like that. Who do you think you are to say Allah will punish me? Go home and leave me to deal with Nadia. I don't need your commotion." Fatima turned away and stared at the cushion on the floor.

"Oh. I'm going, and this time when I say I'm not ever coming back here I mean it." Jamila slammed the door behind her and raced off down the driveway in angry tears as a flashback of her beloved Hassan fighting to stay afloat in their old swimming pool filled her mind.

* * *

Fatima sat on her chair and calmly poured herself mint tea. She knew that Jamila was right, but it made no difference to her as she gleefully sipped her tea.

Nobody gets in the way of my plans or my perfect family.

She'd successfully married off her two sons and one daughter. The only marriage left was Nadia's to her intended husband. The threats to harm Grace remained real and vivid to Nadia and that was Fatima's main intention.

* * *

Upstairs Nadia lay on her bed in tears. Hating herself for her behaviour towards Grace, the love of her life, at sending her away in tears with a fictitious explanation.

Grace couldn't begin to understand that my evil mother will do anything to get her own way. She always does. I love Grace deeply and couldn't live with myself if that devil downstairs harmed her. I can't live in fear in London for the rest of my life and I definitely can't risk Grace's life just for my own contented happiness. I can't!

Nadia had a flashback and remembered the time when her and Zeina were becoming more than just teenage school friends. They had kissed on the lips and felt the warm embrace of each other. Nothing more than that as none were ready to go any further, but they both knew as teenagers that they were falling in love.

They both knew those feelings were real and no one but them would understand it. That was until Fatima noticed they were getting uncomfortably close and she pushed Zeina down the stairs, making it look like an accident.

Zeina broke both legs and didn't come to their

Hidden Evil

house again, she ignored Nadia at school. Nadia knew Fatima had warned Zeina to stay away so she did.

Fatima always got her own way. Nadia wasn't prepared to gamble on her mother's viciousness, only to discover that she had harmed Grace, she couldn't live with that.

What else can I do but ask Grace to go home to Darcy and to safety without me. To get as far away as possible from my vicious mother.

My mother always wins.
Or does she?

Chapter Thirty

Later that evening Grace's phone rang from an unknown number.

"This is my new number but don't ever call me on it. I'll only call you when it's safe to speak," Nadia said in a whisper.

"What? I don't understand. I've spent weeks terrified you were dead and then thinking you'd had your memory erased to find out that you're now going along with that monster's wishes and broke my heart today after all we've been through and now, you're calling me in secret and telling me casually not to call you. What in God's name is going on in your head, Nadia?"

"I know it's difficult for you to understand right now, but I need you to be far away from my mother. She's dangerous and has the means to harm you."

"Why don't you come to me right now and we can leave together?"

"I can't risk putting you in danger, my love."

"She doesn't scare me into leaving without you."

"Listen, I have a plan but I need you to go home and be safe with Darcy. Will you please leave Dubai?"

"What about *you*? I'm worried she'll hurt you again."

"Don't worry about me. She's hurting me emotionally to get her own way but she won't ever hurt me physically. My father won't allow that and she knows it."

"Can we meet so you can tell me your plan before I go?"

"As much as I'd love to hold you in my arms, we must be careful. I can't rest until I know you're out of here. I want you to get on the first plane home tomorrow. Will you please, Grace, just do what I say?"

"Okay."

"Give Darcy a hug from me and tell him I'll see him soon."

"Call me tomorrow when I'm home and you can speak to him and tell him yourself."

"Okay I'll do my best. I need to hang up now. I'll see you both soon. I love you. Bye."

"I love you. Bye."

Grace felt a startled relief at the thought of Nadia coming to her senses and of going home to Darcy but anxious about leaving Nadia behind to deal with Fatima alone.

Grace walked into the kitchen to help herself to a cold beer.

She booked her flight with Emirates direct to Heathrow for the next morning and sent the details to her mother, asking to meet her at the airport with Darcy.

Grace threw everything she owned into her suitcase and sat outside the back of the villa drinking more beer before she retired to bed early with her alarm set.

As she lay in the safehouse bed for the final night, she pondered the events of the last few weeks. Would they ever get over it?

I think I'm losing my mind but Nadia has absolutely already lost hers.

Chapter Thirty-One

Nadia knew Fatima was keen to move things forward and had arranged for Nassir and Nadia to dine at the Burj Al Arab underwater restaurant, whilst she and his mother Huda would meet to plan the wedding. Nadia agreed to dine with Nassir, she was ready to set her own plan in motion.

Nadia elegantly stepped out of Ahmed's Hummer outside the iconic Burj Al Arab hotel. She walked past the decorative fountain towards the tall elegant entrance with her high heels clattering on the marble pavement.

Looking stunningly beautiful in her white laced designer knee-length dress, she smiled as she noticed Nassir standing alone waiting for her looking dapper in his tailor-made navy evening suit with open neck blue and white striped shirt.

"Hi gorgeous, how are you?" Nassir smiled and took her hand to guide her through the lobby and up the escalator passing the copious amounts of gold statues, gold Romanesque pillars that lined the walls.

They glanced into the brightly lit windows as they passed by designer jewellery shops with the world's most expensive watches of every design and brand, to turn right into the small elevator down to the underwater cocktail bar for pre-dinner drinks.

"I'm not so good, handsome, but happy to see you as always." She held his hand until they stood alone inside the elevator.

"Hey what's up?"

"I have a lot to tell you and I'm hoping you'll understand." She pushed her long black hair behind one ear, exposing her green diamond-studded earrings, and neatened her fringe.

The elevator smoothly dipped underground and opened as they were met by a charming man who guided them through the dimly lit arched shell designed entrance to a table in the cocktail bar. They sat on red velvet chairs and ordered non-alcoholic cocktails.

"Tell me, Nadia, what's up?" Nassir asked her when the waiter left to fetch their drinks.

"I'm already married to my wife in London."

"What?" Nassir paused as the information digested. "Oh!" He fell silent again, awaiting her story to unfold.

"I make no apology for my life choices and as much as I've always been fond of you, I need you to know that I can never be your wife."

He gasped. "I agree to that but why are our mothers

meeting this evening to plan our wedding? Do they know about your wife?"

"My mother knows but I'm not sure about yours. I shouldn't be telling you this because my mother is adamant that we should still marry as planned."

"I don't know what to say, Nadia. How terrible for you to be in this situation. I'm so sorry this has happened to you."

"My mother left me no choice but to go along with her scheme, because my wife is still here and I'm worried for her safety, but she's on the first plane out of here tomorrow morning."

He held her hands across the table to comfort her. "How awful for you both. How can I help? What can I do?"

The waiter arrived with their drinks.

"I need a stiff drink. Do you want one?" Nassir asked Nadia.

"Yes, I'll have a gin and tonic please."

Nassir nodded to the waiter. "A large Irish whisky for me please." He turned back to Nadia.

She spoke next. "I need you to tell them you don't want to marry me anymore because you've realised after our meeting tonight, you still love your wife. Will you do that for me?"

He smiled genuinely. "Yes, I can do that, I don't think my mother will believe me but I'll do it for you, because we've always been friends and I'd like to remain on good terms with you. If I can't have you as my wife then I must insist we stay connected."

The waiter arrived with drinks and they both drank quickly.

Nassir nodded at the waiter a second time. "Same again please."

The waiter returned with another round of drinks and asked if they were ready to move to their reserved table inside the plush restaurant. They said they were so he carried the drinks on a tray as they followed him.

Nassir and Nadia admired the colourful array of fish swimming above and around them behind the glass façade.

"I wanted to propose to you tonight under the eyes of the fish." Nassir winked as he sat down facing her.

"And it would've been a spectacular proposal," she replied with a beaming smile.

They ate a full five courses and drank whisky and gin as they planned out when and how to disclose that they wouldn't be getting married after all.

Chapter Thirty-Two

It was near midnight when Nassir and Nadia stood outside the hotel next to the glorious water fountain. Nassir held on to her to help her stand up straight as he hailed his driver from the line of cars and opened the door to help her inside.

"I'm taking you home to make sure you get there safely," Nassir said when he realised how drunk she had become once they were outside in the humid air.

"I'll be okay on my own, thanks." She fell onto the back seat.

He placed her seatbelt on and walked around the other side of the car to enter and instructed the driver to take a diversion to drop her home first.

"Shall I walk you to the door?" Nassir asked in a drunken slur as the car pulled up outside her house.

"No thanks, shush, I can manage." She placed her finger up to her lips and wriggled herself out of the back seat.

"Good night, gorgeous, I hope to see you again soon," he said.

"Good night, handsome, you will."

* * *

Nadia slammed the door shut behind her and clattered up the steps to the front door, where she rummaged through her bag but found no door keys.

"Oh shit," she whispered, remembering she didn't have a set of keys to evil monsters' mansion.

She rang the doorbell and leant on one of the outside pillars contemplating whether to remove her shoes whilst awaiting a maid to open it, but she couldn't decide and eventually a maid arrived in her night gown to quietly let her in.

"I'm so sorry to wake you but I forgot to take a key," Nadia said as she quietly entered the hallway.

"It's okay, madam, best not to wake your mother. Do you need help upstairs?" the maid asked.

"No thanks, you go back to bed and sorry again for waking you."

The maid disappeared to her quarters as Nadia made her way slowly up the polished marble steps holding onto the cast-iron banister with one hand and her high heels in the other. She lost her grip on her shoes and they banged their way back downstairs.

"What time is it?" Fatima asked sleepily, appearing on the landing.

"No idea, Mother," Nadia replied with hiccups.

"Have you been drinking?" Fatima snapped.

"Yep!"

"How dare you come home in this state!"

"This isn't my home," Nadia said, walking further upstairs.

"Who do you think you are to disobey my house rules?"

"I've been celebrating." Nadia chuckled as she reached the top of the stairs, feeling pleased with the evening's achievement.

"Are you engaged?" Fatima said in a calmer voice, standing next to a vase of colourful tulips.

"Why would I get engaged when I'm already married?"

"Huda and I went to great lengths to arrange this evening's dinner for you to accept Nassir's proposal." Fatima grabbed Nadia's arms to stop her from falling.

"Oops! I must be drunk as it's not part of the plan to admit that yet, but I'm not marrying Nassir... not now, not ever." She pulled away from Fatima and swung her arms in the air as she swayed towards the banister and almost fell over it again.

"*Did* he propose?" Fatima held her to keep her steady.

Nadia positioned her face closer to her mother's. "No need. I told him everything you've done to me and how I'm already happily married to Grace. He was quite shocked by your obsession to control my life and extremely concerned over the threats to harm Grace if I didn't go along with your plan."

"You're a stupid little bitch!" Fatima slapped her hard on the cheek as she screamed at her.

Nadia's immediate reaction was defence. She slapped her straight back as she felt the burning sensation on her cheek. Fatima then swung her arm up in an attempt to offer a second slap but Nadia grabbed her hand, and a struggle on the landing ensued.

Fatima suddenly lost her balance and began to fall from the top step. Her slippers lost their grip on the marbled top step as she leant backwards towards the downward stairway, staring wide eyed into Nadia's eyes with absolute fear.

Nadia instinctively reached out to grab her, just before she decided instead to let her fall.

As Fatima tumbled down the long wide staircase, Nadia focused on the tulips bursting eagerly from their vase which too had tumbled to the floor.

Chapter Thirty-Three

Grace woke, startled, before her alarm went off, after having a restless night full of awful dreams, where every eventuality left her alone without Nadia in her future. Grace turned off her alarm and walked into the kitchen to make fresh coffee.

She thought about eating toast for breakfast but didn't feel hungry. Leaving Dubai without Nadia wasn't part of her plan but she'd agreed to go home and take care of Darcy and await further news. Grace could always come back if needed.

She sat outside on the decking next to the outdoor pool drinking her coffee whilst checking her phone constantly, wishing Nadia would call or text her with anything new. She decided to call her mother with updates.

"Hi, it's me, how's things going there?" Grace asked.

"All's good here, darling, but Darcy really misses

you both. You are flying home today still, aren't you? He keeps asking when you'll both be home."

"I'm definitely coming home today, Mom," she said, holding back her frustration.

"What's Nadia doing? When's she coming home?"

"She hasn't called again since yesterday, begging me to fly home immediately, telling me that her mother has threatened to harm me if she doesn't go along with her plan to marry her cousin."

"I know and I can't believe it. Who does her mother think she is to make these vile threats towards you? I agree with Nadia, Grace. She knows her own mother, their family power and connections to make people suffer or disappear. I know you don't want to hear it but it's best you do as she says and come home."

"I know you're both right but I'm so frustrated to leave her here, not knowing what will happen and if I'll ever see her again." Grace sobbed into the phone.

"If I know Nadia, she'll be following you home as soon as she can get on that plane. Keep your chin up, darling, everything will be alright, you'll see and you can always go back if need be. What time shall we pick you up from Heathrow?"

"I'm on the early morning flight, landing at 1.30pm."

"I need to call the school to keep Darcy off, is that okay?"

"Yes please, I'm dying to see him and hold him. I can't imagine how upset he's been without us, but at least he has you and Dad to take care of him. I don't know how I'd cope if it weren't for you two helping us out. I can't thank you enough."

"No need to thank us, that's what parents are for. Besides, we love having Darcy with us and spoil him. Be sure you get on that plane. We'll be waiting as you come out. See you in a few hours, safe journey. I love you."

Grace hung up and sobbed into her hands. She couldn't hold back the tears as the realisation set in further; she was going home alone.

She showered, ordered a taxi and packed up the rest of her belongings through more tears.

Brian arrived back to the house as she was leaving.

"Good to catch you and see you off safely, Grace. Have a good flight home, I wish you all the best." He hugged her.

"You too, Brian. Wishing you a speedy trial and getting back to earning money to buy your home back in Birmingham." She hugged him and stepped into the taxi.

Not until the flight staff prepared for take-off, did Grace place her phone onto aeroplane mode. She waited until the last second, hoping for a call or a text from Nadia that didn't arrive.

Chapter Thirty-Four

Nadia looked down at the bottom of the stairs to see her mother lying in a contorted position in the large dimly lit hallway. Fatima was face up with her left leg under her back.

Nadia immediately sobered up with the shock and ran down the stairs.

"Oh my god! What have I done. What have I done?" Nadia shouted louder and louder until her father appeared in his bedroom doorway, half asleep.

"What's going on, what time is it?" He turned the dimmer switch to light up the landing and wake himself.

Nadia trembled hysterically as she bent over her mother's body.

He rushed downstairs. "Oh no, no."

"She's breathing, she's okay," he said as he checked her pulse and ran to the kitchen to call for an ambulance.

The maids appeared in their long nightgowns and head coverings to see what the commotion was. They all looked concerned for Fatima.

* * *

Mohammed held Nadia as she continued to shake and he shushed her. He was confused and couldn't understand how Fatima had fallen or why she was out of bed so late.

"What happened, Nadia?"

He smelled alcohol and summoned the maids to help him to hide Nadia in her bedroom before the police and paramedics arrived.

"Put her to bed and make sure she stays there. Don't let her out until we've all left. If they catch her in this state, she'll be arrested," Mohammed told the maids then ran back downstairs, passing his wife on the floor, to open the door to the awaiting paramedics.

* * *

The paramedics rushed towards Fatima. They checking her pulse, attached and tied a head and neck brace then gently lifted her onto a stretcher into the ambulance.

The police arrived as the ambulance was leaving the driveway and rolled down the driver-side window to speak to one of the paramedics.

Once the police realised General Mohammad

Hidden Evil

Aktoum was sitting in the back, with his wife on a stretcher, they nodded, turned on the siren, and escorted the ambulance to the Emirates Hospital.

Chapter Thirty-Five

Grace walked past Customs towards the arrivals entrance to find her parents and Darcy.

"Mommy over here!" Darcy shouted, smiling and waving as she appeared.

"Hello everyone. Am I happy to see you all," Grace said as she held them in a long embrace.

"How was your flight, dear?" Susan asked.

"It was good thanks, Mom." Grace smiled and winked, showing her mother that she was doing her best to avoid upsetting Darcy.

Darcy looked disappointed. "How is Momma? Gran said she has to stay in Dubai for work."

"She's fine, sweetheart, and sends all her love and hugs for you. Here's a big kiss and hug from her."

Her father put his arm around Grace's shoulders and took hold of the suitcase with the other. "The car is on the lower-level car park. Come on, let's get you home."

Grace held onto Darcy's hand with a gentle squeeze as they walked towards the car park.

The journey home from Heathrow Airport was pleasant. Grace rolled the window down and was glad of the fresh spring air on her face as she breathed it in and closed her eyes momentarily.

Her father stopped off at a petrol station to buy sandwiches for lunch at Grace's as well as milk and bread, the essentials after time away.

Upon arrival at her front door, Grace became tearful but held them back as she walked into the bright airy hallway, remembering the last time they were all there together, excited for their dream holiday in Dubai.

Her mother put the kettle on as Grace sat with Darcy on her lap, asking him how school was and telling him that he would be back with his friends the next day.

"I miss my friends, Mommy, but I missed you and Momma more, that's why Gran said I can take a day off to come to the airport to get you."

"I love you so much and we both missed you more," Grace told him with another big hug.

"Tea and yummy sandwiches. Eat it all up, Darcy, then you can watch your favourite movie again," Gran said as she placed the tray onto the side table next to him.

When Darcy sat near the TV, his grandmother moved out of his earshot onto the couch next to Grace.

"That mother of hers is vicious. I can't imagine

what type of childhood she's had to be so vile," Susan whispered.

"You can't blame everything on someone's childhood, Mom. She's evil and that's that."

"How is Nadia? Have you spoken to her since yesterday?" Robert asked.

Grace held her tears back again. "No, I thought she'd call me before I boarded but she must be with her mother and couldn't get a chance."

"Look, she will call you soon and be home in no time, I'm sure of it," Susan said.

"I hope so. I miss her so much and have no idea how she'll be after the trauma from the clinic on top of her mother's control."

"I didn't want to say but you look exhausted and you've lost some weight. Do you want to go and lie down for a while? I'll take Darcy to the shops and get dinner in."

"Definitely not, I need to be awake in case Nadia calls. I'll come to the shops with you both and get some fresh air. It seems like months since I've done a shop for food or anything normal."

Grace called her office to catch up on client developments and informed them she was home but would need more time off. She had no intention of trying to handle the grind of corporate law yet.

Later that evening after dinner, kindly cooked by Susan, Grace became more anxious that Nadia still hadn't called.

"Do you want me to stay the night? Your father can go home and collect me tomorrow," Susan asked.

"I'll be okay thanks, Mom. I need to show some form of normality to Darcy and I'm sure Nadia will call me later."

Her parents left after goodbyes at the doorway and they drove off into the night.

Grace put Darcy to bed and sat with the TV on mute, drinking red wine, awaiting anxiously for her phone to ring. She tried to read a book but couldn't concentrate.

Hours passed but still no call came. Exhausted Grace paced the living room then eventually fell asleep on the couch, only to wake cold and lonely in the small hours of the morning. She tried to stay awake as long as she could but the wine took over and she fell back to sleep.

* * *

She woke early as the sunlight dipped through the living room curtains.

She jumped up and checked her phone but no missed calls. She was both relieved that she hadn't missed a call but frustrated that there hadn't been one.

Her head was thumping as she entered the kitchen and made coffee to sober up.

She sat at the kitchen table and the tears came.

She had no idea how long she had been crying but was startled when Darcy appeared in the doorway, rubbing his eyes.

"Why are you sad, Mommy?"

Grace wiped her cheeks dry and smiled as she hugged him. "I'm tired and miss Momma, just like you do. Let's get your pancakes on. You can mix it with me, okay?"

"Yes, I'm very hungry."

"You're *always* hungry." Grace laughed as she sat him on the counter and helped him make pancakes.

After breakfast they got ready and Grace walked Darcy to school. The same familiar walk she'd done for years felt strange.

She felt robotic as the other parents greeted her and asked if she'd had a nice holiday. She didn't know what to say and was unprepared, but smiled back at them all as she lied, saying it had been lovely.

"I'm so jealous. I'd love to go to Dubai and see all that glitz and luxury," Janet's mother said.

"It certainly is a glitzy city," Zoe's dad agreed.

"It's very hot there," Grace replied, trying to leave the group of parents at the gates as fast as she could.

She walked home clutching her phone, awaiting the call but it didn't come.

Back at home, she cleared up the plates solemnly and put them in the dishwasher. She held the wine glass from the previous night and instead of placing it in the dishwasher, she decided to drink a bit more, so opened another bottle from the wine rack. The two empty bottles went into the recycle bin.

Upstairs in their bedroom, Grace unpacked her suitcase and sipped the wine, still waiting for the call. Afterwards she lay on the bed and more tears came.

* * *

By mid-morning she was on her next bottle. She was out of control; the call still hadn't come.

Back downstairs she began to open the mound of mail that had been delivered in their absence. Almost a month had passed so it was laborious to sort through. She threw most of it in the bin without opening it.

* * *

By lunchtime she was in the fridge eating cheese biting it from the block, without bothering to cut it and opening another bottle of wine. She stumbled into the garden to get some fresh air but the air mixed with too much wine made her feel nauseous.

She checked her phone again but no missed calls. Anxiously she checked the ringtone was still on high and the vibration was activated. She was too drunk to not call Nadia.

She pressed the number and listened on speaker for it to be answered. No answer. She tried again, no answer. Again, no answer.

"Where are you, where the fuck are you?" she

shouted into the phone as a neighbour appeared over the fence to see what was up.

"Grace, are you alright?"

"I'm not alright, no!"

"Can I help you with anything? What's up?"

"I'm going in. I'm alright," Grace replied in a slur and waved her hands in the air as she stumbled back inside.

She poured another glass and sat on the couch and more tears came.

A loud bang on the front door startled her as she woke up from the couch.

"Grace, open the door!" Susan banged again.

Grace opened the door. Her mother stood there, with Darcy in hand looking horrified.

"The school called me to collect him, what's going on? Are you drunk in the middle of the afternoon?"

"I am definitely drunk," she slurred as she fell back onto the wall.

"Oh Grace, you must stop this. It's not doing any one of us any good. The school tried calling you but when you didn't answer or turn up at the gates, they rang me," Susan said as she helped Grace into the living room and back onto the couch.

"No! I didn't hear my phone ring, what if I've missed a call from Nadia?" Grace slurred as she picked up her phone and checked the missed calls, with one eye closed. None from Nadia, just three from school.

"I can't believe you missed picking him up. I'm really worried about you, Grace. You must pull yourself together, this can't go on."

"How can I pull myself together when I haven't heard from Nadia? I don't know if she's alright or ever coming home."

"For God's sake. It's only been a day since you got back. You know this is unacceptable behaviour, you have responsibilities. I'm sure she'll call when she can and that she's fine now she's out of that clinic and planning to be home soon."

"I'm sorry, Mom. I'm so sorry, Darcy, sweetheart," she said as realisation set in and she grabbed Darcy and hugged him.

Her mother shook her head. "Get in the shower and try to sober up. I'll make you a coffee, and a sandwich for Darcy."

"Thanks, Mom, I don't know what I'd do without you," Grace slurred with agreement as she went up to shower and sober up, feeling hopeless yet again.

Susan poured the rest of the bottle into the sink in disgust and put the empties into the recycle bin, noticing three already in there.

Grace was quiet upstairs as her mother made the sandwich for Darcy and prepared black strong coffee for her.

* * *

Hidden Evil

After half an hour her mother went upstairs to see why Grace was taking so long in the shower and found her lying across the bed, breathing heavily in her drunken state and fully clothed with the shower still running, which she switched off.

She decided to leave her to sleep and placed a blanket over her and took her phone downstairs to wait for a call from Nadia.

No call came all evening, so her mother decided to stay overnight and put Darcy to bed. Her daughter was in no fit state, mentally or physically, to cope alone.

When will this all end?

Chapter Thirty-Six

Nadia sat at her mother's hospital bedside in the ICU. Wires were attached to machines bleeping and nurses were checking Fatima's vitals every thirty minutes. Her left leg and both her arms were in plaster, her head bandaged and in a head and neck brace. Fatima was in a coma with the doctors unable to say if she would ever wake up.

Did I want this to happen? Nadia thought. *No. Did I want my mother to suffer? Yes, but not like this. I'm no better than she is. I must be her daughter to be this evil. I should've caught her before she fell. I was drunk and I've lost my mind but I know I couldn't be this evil if she hadn't given birth to me... could I?*

Fatima's lifelong friend Huda arrived, looking glamorous holding a vase full of gladioli in a beautiful arrangement.

"Hello Nadia, darling. What did the doctors say about her waking up? Will she be okay?" Huda asked, looking worried and flustered.

"They don't know yet, they're monitoring her and hoping for the best. We'll have to pray and wait to find out."

"What happened? Your father called to tell me that she's here."

"She fell down the stairs in the dark in the early hours of this morning."

"What was she doing in the dark?"

"I don't know. I was in bed asleep after your son bought me home last night, relieved that I won't be marrying him."

"What? Why not? A wedding is planned. What happened?"

"I told him I'm already married and spending my life with my wife in London. He was very understanding but totally shocked you hadn't mentioned that I had a wife." Nadia smirked.

"Why would I tell anyone about your dirty secret living against Allah with a woman?" Huda scoffed and left the room in disgust.

"Except it's not dirty, you bitch, or a SECRET!" Nadia yelled after her.

Nadia stared at her lifeless mother's body full of tubes without feeling any remorse. She took her purse out of her handbag and marched off to the canteen to find food, now her appetite and mind were restored.

She didn't need to worry about her meddling vicious mother anymore.

Time to get on with her life and return to London.

* * *

Hidden Evil

Feeling calmer after her delicious lunch of Arabic delights, Nadia went back to her mother's room to collect her handbag. She was about to enter the room when she saw Huda sitting at her mother's bedside whispering.

Huda didn't notice as Nadia held back patiently in the doorway so as not to disturb her and to listen in to her whispers.

She wasn't a fan of Huda or her righteous remarks but she respected her devotion to Fatima as her best friend and knew it was her own mother who had plotted for their children to marry. Huda as usual went along with everything Fatima told her to, in order to keep the peace. Fatima controlled Huda the same way she controlled everyone else in her life.

"How can I live without you, Fatima?" Huda was saying. "I can't survive this cruel life alone. I've only ever loved you and wouldn't know how to start a life without you, my love. Please wake up and come back to me. I need to hold you in my arms like always and make love with you." Huda whispered whilst squeezing Fatima's hand.

Nadia stormed into the room. "What the hell's going on here between you two, Huda?"

"Nothing's going on between us." Huda blushed.

"I can't believe you two have been secret lovers all these years and still find the need to lie to me about mother's cancer to pull on my heart, get me over here, then abduct me and force me against my will into a mental facility. Then you kidnapped my son and arrested my wife who spent two terrifying nights in prison thinking I'd been killed. How in the name of Allah can you of all people believe it's abnormal to be attracted to the same sex? When you both know how unavoidable and normal it is for people like us to feel this way?" Nadia raged as she tried to digest the information.

"I didn't agree with Fatima to take you there or do anything she did, that was all her idea. I told her it was wrong to try to convert you, but it's not normal to be like us if we're going against Allah who'll punish us for our wickedness."

"You're a total hypocrite living a lie and having your screwed-up righteous values imposed onto me whilst you commit adultery, allowing your husbands to be blindly oblivious to your own infidelity."

"We didn't have a choice, Nadia, because it's a criminal offence and we wanted children and a normal life that Allah respects. It's difficult to live with this huge secret, but we do for the sake of Allah, the law, our husbands and our families. I can't imagine not having my children or have my family disown me or having friends look down on me, knowing I'm not normal like they are."

Nadia shook her head. "Oh my god. I'm really trying to understand your situation, Huda. I know how the law here frightens people who are different and the shame our families and culture puts on those who dare to come out, but it's totally different for me. I live in London where it's legal. I have a wife and I'm not ashamed. I have a child. I'm happy at work where my colleagues know I'm a lesbian and respect me for choosing to own my life. All I ever wanted was for my mother to accept me for whom I am, that's all.

"I know I can't live here and be free from the shackles you both have, but why would she deny me my life because she couldn't have it herself? Why can't she accept me as I am, especially now I've found out that she *really* does understand me more than I ever knew?"

"You'd have to ask your mother those questions now you know our dirty secret, but I know two reasons. Firstly, she wants you back in Dubai living near her, especially as she's getting older, so you'd have to conform to our societies values and law to be accepted. Secondly, she's jealous that you have everything that she couldn't have."

"What? How can a mother be jealous of her own daughter's happiness. She truly is EVIL." Nadia only heard the second reason, because she already knew the first. She grabbed her handbag from the bed and stormed out the room, shaking with rage.

She raced out of the hospital and took a taxi back to Emirates Hills, having called Jamila to meet her there with her passport she was keeping safe for her.

Chapter Thirty-Seven

Upon arrival at the mansion, Nadia was still shaking as she entered by the front door that one of the maids opened.

"Are you not feeling well madam?" the maid asked.

"I've never felt better my whole life. Thanks for asking." Nadia stormed upstairs to pack her things into her suitcase and wait for Jamila to arrive with her passport.

She was frantically throwing her belongings into the suitcase when she heard the doorbell ring.

"I'm upstairs, sis, come up!" Nadia shouted.

Jamila arrived at the bedroom door to witness her big sister shaking enraged and frantic.

"What's up? Why are you packing? Aren't you staying to marry Nassir as arranged?"

"For fuck's sake. To think I'd almost succumbed in that prison clinic to obey Mother and give up my life in London with Grace. Well, I may have lost my mind intermittently but I'm definitely not staying. I told Nassir everything last night."

"That was a terrible idea! Your secret should remain only in the family, as all secrets have."

Nadia stopped packing and stood with her hands on her hips, facing Jamila. "Don't make me laugh. Do you want to know the biggest hidden secret in this righteous vicious family?"

"I know all the secrets, sis, none have got past me. I'm the one who stayed here and live the life Mother planned for me, remember."

"Really! Did you know Mother and Huda are LOVERS?"

Jamila burst out laughing. "Now you've definitely lost your blooming mind."

"I've just caught Huda declaring her undying love for Mother. She admitted it and told me how JEALOUS Mother is that I'm happily living her dream life. Our mother is FUCKING EVIL personified."

"No! I don't believe it." Jamila sat slowly on the bed. "Shush, stop shouting, Nadia, the maids will hear you."

"I don't give a damn if the *neighbourhood* hears me, she's not getting away with her deception anymore."

"Calm down and listen to yourself. Think how this will effect Father and his job. Think about our brothers and the whole family. How this will devastate the façade Mother has built for us all." Jamila pulled Nadia onto the bed and put an arm around her to comfort and calm her down.

"It's not right what she's doing to me." Nadia sat with her head in her hands, trembling with rage.

"Sis, I know, and you're right! She shouldn't have done any of the vile things she's done to all of us all our lives. I know you're angry right now and want vengeance, but that's not you, is it. You're not that person and never will be. It's just your anger surfacing at her wickedness after what she's put you through. Sometimes life isn't fair, is it. By going back to Grace and living your chosen happy life is enough to destroy Mother. That's if she ever wakes up from the coma.

"She's paid all that money to wipe your mind and tried to deceive you into conforming to her demands. She's failed miserably and Allah has given his wrath on her, that's enough revenge." Jamila held her tighter.

"She'll wake up, I feel it, because she's the devil in disguise. She'll never give up her control of us and ruining all our lives."

"Stop that talk. Mother is vicious and controlling, often out of love. I can't say she's the devil in disguise. You're raging and need to calm down."

"Do you want to know about my rage? It's dark and growing inside me, like a big black lump of burning tar. It started in my chest and now it's in my gut and I hope it never comes out. I feel no other way to describe her. I don't desire the acceptance of the devil and can't believe how it used to be so important to me. That's me done." Nadia looked down as she pulled herself away from Jamila.

"What was she doing up that early anyway?" Jamila asked.

"Probably plotting her next spell on this family or how to harm Grace and get away with it." Nadia avoided eye contact. She had no intention of declaring she was part of a scuffle that ended with their mother at the bottom of the stairs.

"She wouldn't harm Grace. She only threatened that as part of your treatment. Would she?"

"That's insanity isn't it though. That's not part of any treatment, sis, to threaten and blackmail me emotionally is it? She harmed our teenage lovers didn't she! They're lucky to be alive. She was the devil warming up and now she's completely failed with me. Only Allah knows what she's capable of when she wakes up and gets back home."

Jamila checked her watch. "Come with me to fetch the girls from school. I don't want to leave you alone in this state."

Nadia reluctantly agreed and picked up her handbag to go.

They walked to the car, mentally exhausted and still in shock at the knowledge of another hidden secret and how the family's lives have been affected by it.

"Now we know why they went on all those trekking holidays in Europe. They always suggested trips that nobody wanted to go on so they could be alone," Jamila said.

Nadia smirked. "I guarantee the liars didn't do any trekking."

"What about all those spa trips over in Oman they go to every month? I mean friends often go to those ladies-only places to get away together, relax and catch up without husbands and kids in tow. I go with my friends when I can. It's beautiful over there, five-star luxury pampering for three days solid."

"I know and that's how they hid it so well; nobody's suspicious of it. I'm still in shock but it doesn't bother me. I understand why they hid that they're lovers."

"Father has had a mistress for years and now we know why," Jamila reminded her.

"If only they'd told us their secret when we became grown women. I don't care what they get up to and understand why they've had to hide it living here. It's not that Mother has hidden it so much as she's vilified me extensively over the past seven years since she found out about Grace, that's what angers me."

* * *

Jamila pulled up at the school and went in to fetch the girls, leaving Nadia still angry in the airconditioned car.

"Hi girls did you have a nice day at school?" Nadia asked, attempting a fake smile, when they returned.

"Yes, thank you, Auntie Nadia," they echoed with smiles, oblivious to the last few hours of devastation she had been through.

"I've been to see Grandma Fatima in hospital today. She's not well and I haven't had time to cook so we'll go to your favourite place to eat pizza, okay?" Jamila smiled in relief that she couldn't discuss Fatima and Huda in front of the girls, giving her a rest from all the tangled memories popping into her mind.

"Yay pizza," the girls echoed. They'd only heard 'pizza'.

Nadia and Jamila laughed together at the girls' answer, ignoring that Grandma was in hospital.

Chapter Thirty-Eight

After the restaurant, Jamila dropped her daughters home and drove herself and Nadia back to the hospital. It was getting dark around five thirty and the streets were packed with rush-hour traffic.

Drivers dodged lanes and beeped horns to get by. It was always exhausting driving at rush hour and Jamila wished she had missed it but her mind wasn't focused on the time of day.

She wanted to see if their mother had woken and try to calm Nadia's anger as they began to accept the secret.

They entered the hospital and the porter parked the car as they walked along the corridors to their mother's ICU room. Upon approach they noticed the blinds open and asked to close them from the bright lights in the corridor.

The nurse closed the blinds and gave them an update on their mother.

"She's highly medicated to ease the pain but we've

seen no progress this evening. It's early days and she's recovering from her body's stress of the broken bones, fractures and bruises."

"Has she had a brain scan?" Nadia asked.

"Yes, she had that this afternoon along with an MRI to check for any skull fractures and organ damage. Let me show you the results." The nurse rummaged through the clipped paperwork hung at the bottom of the bed. "Looks like your mother has normal brainwaves and no fluid leakage as far as we can tell. The coma has been brought on by narrowing of blood vessels but she is stable so we're not worried. We'll know more when she wakes if there's any trauma damage or cognitive impairment."

The nurse read off the medical notes. "She has twelve fractures in both her ribs and five fractures in her right leg that will all heal in time, and her organs are working fine without any aid."

"Thank you, it seems she's very lucky, after such a bad stumble down those marble stairs," Jamila replied with a tinge of optimism.

"I agree she's very lucky and needs your prayers for full recovery." The nurse smiled as she checked her alarm on her hip that was buzzing for assistance. "I'll be back outside the room by the desk after I've answered this if you need anything more." She hurried out the room and closed the door behind her.

"That's good news, Nadia, isn't it?" Jamila asked with a tired smile.

"Great," Nadia replied without conviction. She felt

zero remorse or empathy for her mother and couldn't hide it from Jamila.

"Come on now, it's our mother, try to be pleased," Jamila insisted.

"Okay I'll try. I'm going to fetch water while you sit with her, okay?"

Nadia couldn't wait to get out the room away from her mother. She walked to the canteen and purchased two bottles of cold water then back to the room the long way around.

All the time she was feeling scared that her mother would wake up but also scared that she wouldn't. She couldn't decide how she would feel either way but dreaded both scenarios for different reasons.

When she arrived back at the room, Father was sitting the other side of the bed to Jamila.

"Hello Father, how are you?" Nadia asked with a wry smile.

"I'm better now Jamila just told me that the doctors are confident that your mother will recover. Tell me what happened last night, Nadia."

Nadia had been dreading this conversation because she knew her family could detect her lying but she put on a brave face and acted out the story she had prepared earlier.

"I'd got home from dinner with Nassir and as I walked upstairs carrying my shoes, they dropped back downstairs and banged, startling Mother awake. I quickly went inside my room before she saw me, because I didn't want her to see I'd been drinking, especially with all that prescribed clinic medication I'm on.

"I knew she'd worry and moan at my irresponsibility as usual. Then I heard banging and I thought something else had fallen downstairs so I went out to see. When I saw it was Mother on the hallway floor, I rushed to her saying 'what have I done', meaning I've woken her up drunk and I felt terrible." Nadia finished off with her head down to avoid their eyes.

"Come here, love. It's not anyone's fault. Don't blame yourself. Your mother can be clumsy as we all know and accidents happen. Don't be sad." He comforted her with his big strong arms making her feel devilish, lying like her mother.

They sat on chairs around the bed for a few hours, awaiting any movement.

"It's getting late and I'm tired with worry. I'm going home now to catch Mo before he retires and get a good night sleep so I'll see you both tomorrow, okay?" Jamila announced.

'Yes, we should all go home and get good sleep, ready for shifts at Mother's bedside tomorrow in case she wakes up to strangers and misses a familiar face," Father suggested.

"What if she wakes up in the night and nobody's here that she knows?" Nadia asked.

Father nodded. "You're right, I'll stay overnight on a camp bed and you two go home to rest and come back early to take over watch."

"Don't you have early meetings tomorrow?" Jamila asked him.

Hidden Evil

Nadia felt obliged to offer. "I'll stay and keep watch. I have nothing to rush home for or get up for, so you two go home get some sleep and carry on your busy days tomorrow. You can then come swap with me once you're ready."

They all agreed.

Father asked the night staff for a camp bed for Nadia and the trio hugged each other goodnight.

Chapter Thirty-Nine

With the room silent, Nadia pondered over staying awake on the chair or sleeping on the made-up camp bed. She decided on the former for now. Although exhausted mentally, she didn't feel tired enough to sleep yet.

She listened to her mother breathing slowly, looking very peaceful and relaxed, and remembered her looking that way, back when they often napped together in the afternoons when she was a small child.

Nadia immediately had an epiphany, realising she didn't have any fond memories of her mother except watching her sleep peacefully.

That can't be true. Come on, Nadia, there must be other treasured memories of Mother to dig inside your mind and find, or has the prison clinic erased them all?

Prison clinic, yes, that was all Mother's doing.

I refuse to feel sorry for her looking helpless or bother to remember her in a good light.

My mind is hollow with exhaustion.

I can't see anything good in her. She's an evil monster and always has been. That's all I remember. She's a controlling parasite that never leaves my mind, bringing me fear, misery, heartache and horror and not just to me but everyone and everything she touches.

She's the devil's friend and I HATE her. If only she'd stay asleep forever and leave us all to get on with our lives and be happy!

Deep breath... in and out, in and out...

Nadia lost control of her mind momentarily. She stood and walked next to the bed, placed one hand firmly over her mother's mouth, and pinched her nostrils hard together with the other hand.

Her mother didn't move before she took her last breath. It was easy!

The alarm on the machine next to the bed blared, bringing Nadia back to reality and what she had just done. She jumped onto the camp bed and pulled the covers over herself fully clothed.

When the lights went on and hospital staff rushed into the room, Nadia sat up and wiped her eyes, as if from sleeping.

A nurse pulled Nadia off the bed and summoned her to quickly go outside the room, making space at the bed in order to resuscitate Fatima.

* * *

"Code blue, room eight," a young female doctor shouted outside the room then gave instructions to the team as she jumped upon the side of the bed kneeling next to Fatima and began intensive manual continuous compressions with both hands to the chest.

Another doctor pulled the ventilation rescue pod mask attached to the wall and placed it over Fatima's nose and mouth, making sure not to over ventilate.

A third doctor moved swiftly to seal any openings that might detract the oxygen going in and squeeze oxygen into Fatima's mouth.

A fourth doctor placed a back board under Fatima to allow better resistance for the manual compressions.

A fifth doctor operated the monitor and prepared the electronic defibrillator.

They worked with precision awaiting the code team to arrive.

Three code expert doctors arrived with one taking over the manual compressions, relieving the young female doctor.

The next code expert placed the pads attached to the defibrillator onto Fatima's chest as the third expert prepared to place the defibrillator pulses onto Fatima's chest in a final attempt to get her back to life.

"Let's defibrillate hundred and fifty joules, everyone clear oxygen, clear now," the code captain instructed his anxious team awaiting results.

The code captain pushed the button to release the electrical surge into Fatima. No response. Everyone returned to manual compressions and oxygen pod to two minutes.

"Again, at hundred and fifty joules, everyone clear oxygen, clear now."

He pushed the button to release the electrical surge

into Fatima. No response was monitored. The machines bleeped and everyone went back to their positions to aid a response, working with intensity for two minutes before the final defibrillate.

"Increase to two hundred and fifty joules, everyone clear oxygen, clear now."

He pushed the button a third time to release a stronger electrical surge.

Fatima flatlined.

"Time of death ten sixteen pm," the code captain announced.

The team packed away the apparatus and prepared the room for Ghusl Mayyit, the washing of the body by female family members.

The team remained in despair at losing a patient in their care and settled Fatima's body on the bed as the code captain walked to the visitors' room to deliver the outcome to Nadia.

* * *

Nadia looked towards the entrance of the room and saw the solemn doctor walk in. She knew already what he was going to say.

"I am sorry for your loss, madam. My team and I did all we could to save your mother, may she rest in peace with Allah."

"Oh my god, no." Nadia fainted, falling towards the doctor who grabbed her and sat her on a chair, waiting for her to retain her balance. A woman came in just behind the captain and quickly offered water and held the bottle as Nadia sipped it slowly.

"Would you like to lie down, dear?" the woman asked.

"No thank you I'll be fine here." Nadia looked down without shedding a tear as her mind absorbed the consequences of her actions.

"Can I call someone?" the woman asked.

"I'll call my sister, she'll come."

The doctor and woman left Nadia alone in the room to stare at the floor.

I'll have to tell them I did it. I suffocated my own mother! It was me. I wanted her gone from my life forever. She traumatised me into it without any regret or remorse.

They'll know it was me, won't they? People don't just die like that. I'll have to confess I did it.

The doctors will come in soon with the police and arrest me. I'll wait here a bit longer before making the call to Jamila.

I feel no sadness or loss, no revenge or glee, nothing. I only know that I won't ever miss my mother.

I didn't want it this way, I didn't want to be her killer but she drove me to it, didn't she!

Chapter Forty

A few minutes later the woman reappeared in the visiting room to check on Nadia.

"I've made you a cup of tea, before you go and see your mother. Have you called anyone yet to come?"

"Thank you. I'll drink the tea and then call my sister."

"Would you like me to call her for you? I can use your phone."

"Please. I can't seem to find the words."

"That's quite normal, dear. Nobody wants to be the bearer of such bad news."

Nadia handed her the phone after searching for the number.

The woman smiled as she pressed the dial key and listened to the ringtone whilst she prepared to speak.

* * *

"Hi what's up?" Jamila wondered why Nadia was calling so late.

"Good evening, madam. I'm Amina the bereavement counsellor from the hospital. I'm here with your sister. I'm so sorry to inform you that your mother has sadly passed away."

"What? No, no." Jamila burst into tears.

Her husband Mo woke to her sobs and took the phone. "Hello, who is this?"

"I'm Amina a bereavement counsellor from hospital calling to inform your wife that her mother has sadly passed away, may she rest in peace."

"Oh no." He paused. "Is Nadia with you? Is she alright?"

"She's in shock, sitting with me now. That's why I called."

"Okay thank you. We're on our way. Tell her to stay there please." He hung up and comforted Jamila before calling his father-in-law.

"Your sister is on her way. Drink your tea, dear," Amina said.

Nadia sipped the hot sweet mint tea and felt the warmth surround her mouth as it smoothly passed through her dry throat. She was already feeling better, avoiding the call to say mother was dead and not falling into confessing yet!

* * *

Hidden Evil

The whole family soon arrived and met Nadia in the visiting room, where they all sat together grieving and hugging each other. Amina made more tea, answering questions about the passing and how it had happened.

Nadia remained silent as she listened to Amina tell the story after reading the doctors' notes and preparing to make the passing of a loved one sound more pleasant than it was.

It was a perfect death; she passed away quietly in her sleep with her daughter sleeping in the camp bed, so she wasn't alone and must have felt happy by her daughter's presence before Allah took her with him. According to Amina.

A nurse arrived to inform them that Fatima was ready to be bathed.

Jamila, Nadia and Fatima's daughters-in-law walked in silence into the room. The staff had laid out scissors, cotton wool, three buckets of lukewarm water with mittens, cloths and essence. Along with the two shroud sheets, one to use during washing and the other to envelop her body afterwards.

Nadia, being the eldest, began the religious ritual as written in the Quran. She placed cotton wool into Fatima's ears, mouth and nostrils to prevent the water getting in. Then she meticulously cut off the nightgown with scissors as the others cover Fatima's body with a shroud.

They tilted the covered body onto its left side to begin washing from the right side first. Nadia poured the water over the body; face, hands and feet, while the others soaped with precision. Then they tilted the body to its right side and washed from the left side.

They washed Fatima's hair, teeth, gums, lips and nostrils gently whilst maintaining her privacy and dignity.

The bathing was done three times using three separate buckets of water, the first two using soap and a separate essence and the final wash was the rinse. Then gently removed the cotton wool and the wet shroud, dabbing the body of excess water and replaced it with a dry one, wrapping it slowly but tightly around the body.

Fatima was ready for the family to enter the lowly lit room smelling of essence to offer their prayers. The men walked in silence to the room arriving at the tidy bedside without any tubes or machines. Fatima looked peaceful, they all agreed.

Her father pointed. "What's that mark on her mouth?"

Nadia couldn't open her mouth to confess even if she wanted to speak out and say it was the imprint of her fingernail.

"That was the oxygen pod sealed tight to keep her airways clear for easier breathing," Amina replied in low voice.

Phew that was close. I didn't think of that! It wasn't on her mouth earlier, was it.

Islam doesn't agree with autopsies unless they suspect foul play or the dead person is unidentifiable. If there's no suspicion of foul play then I'm free for now. They all look so sad and hopeless looking at Mother.

Hidden Evil

It's better that I wait to confess.

After an hour in the room reminiscing, the relatives became restless and started to leave one by one. Nadia instinctively wanted to leave before they came back to see Mother, to run outside and hide her shame, but she wanted to show her respect to her loving family and Islamic custom.

Everyone had gone home and left Nadia and her father alone at the bedside.

He squeezed her hand. "I'm happy you stayed, love. She'd be happy to know that you'd forgiven her and stayed to be with her to pass peacefully. I'm certain she knew her eldest daughter was by her bedside."

Nadia remained silent as she squeezed his hand whilst screaming inside.

I didn't forgive her and I never will.

She's the devil who deserved what she had coming to her, but I didn't stay behind to suffocate her. I didn't plan that. It just happened, like she willed me to do it.

Her father drove them home and Nadia went straight to bed after being hugged by all the maids in turn offering their condolences.

Nadia slept blissfully without any hint of what had happened earlier on her mind.

Chapter Forty-One

Grace woke with a blinding headache as the sun shone into her eyes through a crack in the bedroom curtains. She began to panic as she searched for her phone but couldn't find it. She had no idea what time it was.

She used the toilet and went quickly downstairs to look for it there but failed to find it. The kitchen clock displayed 07.00, her usual waking time.

She heard her mother cough upstairs as she was entering the bathroom and closed the door. Grace had a blurry flashback, remembering how wrecked she was the previous day in front of her mother and forgetting to fetch Darcy from school. She cringed at her behaviour being out of control.

She went back upstairs to wake Darcy up for breakfast and ask her mother if she had seen her phone.

"Wake up, sleepy head, it's time for pancakes," Grace whispered to Darcy.

He woke up to a big hug and jumped out of bed as if ready to eat.

As they walked by the bathroom, Mother came out looking glamorous as always.

"You're looking like crap this morning," Susan told Grace.

"Don't rub it in, Mom. I'm sorry for my behaviour yesterday. I'm totally stressed out but I can't use that to forgive myself. I'm worried about Nadia but I won't be drinking again because it just makes me feel worse."

Susan seemed sympathetic. "I have no idea why anyone resorts to drinking alcohol during traumatic times but we do it to block out the madness in our minds."

Grace blushed. "I'll be focusing on Darcy and his needs, no need to worry. Thanks for staying over and helping me out."

They went downstairs into the bright sunny yellow kitchen and cooked breakfast together.

"I can't find my phone. Have you seen it anywhere, Mom?" Grace asked casually as they tucked into a delicious breakfast of bacon and eggs with strong coffee, whilst Darcy enjoyed pancakes.

"I slept with it on my pillow in case Nadia called but she didn't, nobody called you. Here it is." She took it out of her dressing gown pocket and handed it to Grace.

* * *

Susan drove them to school and took Darcy to the gates because Grace wasn't ready to face any parents or teachers, feeling irresponsible and dreadful with a hangover.

Susan and Grace arrived back home and cleaned house before going shopping to buy food and drinks ready for Nadia's return. Grace trying her best not to keep looking at her phone for messages or showing how worried she was.

"You've been quite normal today, Grace. Well done for trying to act your old self but I'm not buying it."

"I'm trying but I keep seeing Nadia's eyes dark with rage. I'm really worried about the treatment she's had at the clinic. There's no telling what's going on in her mind."

"Don't try to analyse her, Grace. We'll know more when she gets home."

"I don't know but I felt her rage at the spa last time I saw her and when she called me later, I could hear both rage and fear in her voice. She's making one decision and then another. She tells me one minute to go home and forget about her and then calls me to say she's concocted a plan to come home soon. What *is* her plan?" Grace sighed and sat at the kitchen table, gulping more water for hydration.

"I hope she calls you soon to put all our minds at rest. I'm just glad you and Darcy are home safe."

Grace's phone vibrated on the kitchen table. "It's Nadia!" Grace picked up.

"Hi, Grace. How's things? Did you get home okay?" Nadia asked in a chirpy tone.

"We did but I'm so worried about you. What's

happening? What's your plan to leave and come home?"

"My plan was just to tell Nassir the truth, which I did, and come home but then Mother fell downstairs and was rushed to hospital. She passed away last night." Nadia spoke like she was talking of a TV character's demise in a soap opera not her own mother.

"What? Oh my god. I'm so sorry."

Susan piped in. "What's happening?"

"Fatima passed away last night," Grace told her.

"Oh no."

"I've got to stay to help Father arrange the funeral but I'll be home straight afterwards. I miss you both so much. Give Darcy a hug for me."

"Of course, we miss you too. How are you holding up?" Grace asked.

"I'm fine but I don't like funerals so that's getting me down a bit."

"Nobody likes funerals." Grace frowned at her strange response.

"I know." Nadia chuckled.

"Where are you now? Are you alone or is someone with you?"

"I'm with Jamila and Father at the registry collecting the death certificate. We need it to get things moving. She'll be buried today."

"Gosh that's quick. Stay with your family as long as you need to," Grace replied, surprised at Nadia's urgency to bury her mother.

"Muslims must be buried within twenty-four hours

after death," Nadia replied as if quoting a divorce law to one of her clients.

"Ah I remember you telling me that." Grace paused.

"We've got the certificate so we're off now to arrange collection of the body from the hospital morgue. I love you both, see you soon, love you," Nadia chirped into the phone.

"We love you too. Sending hugs and thinking of you all, take care." Grace hung up and stared into her phone.

"Poor girl, losing her mother so young," Susan said.

"I know. It's so awful. I just can't imagine losing you, Mom, but she seemed cold and totally unbothered."

"She's still in shock. At least she called and you can put your mind at rest that she's coming home soon."

"She seemed weird though."

"There are no rules on grieving, darling, we all accept death in various ways. She'll be fine and her family will take care of each other. That's what families are for. I'll make us a cup of tea before we collect Darcy."

Susan stood to put the kettle on then arranged the fancy white cups onto a tray next to the matching teapot and milk jug ready to take into the garden, where the sun shone bright awaiting them.

Chapter Forty-Two

Mohammed drove them to the funeral parlour to arrange the ceremony and burial without speaking. He was still numb from the idea of his wife being dead.

Jamila sat with her head down whilst Nadia excitedly watched the glitzy buildings pass by along the highway and marvelled at the density of people going about their lives on a normal day, just like hers.

Nadia and Jamila sat in the waiting area whilst their father discussed the ceremony and burial, which was to begin at 18.00 that evening. They drove home quietly discussing who to call and what further arrangements they'd need as they approached Emirates Hills.

Father telephoned the caterers and then they all proceeded to call family and friends with updates, before writing a list of items for Ahmed the driver to fetch for the mourners after the burial.

The maids began to prepare the home as they waited for the caterers to arrive and give them further instructions.

Jamila drove home to prepare herself and arrive with her husband at the morgue.

The caterers soon arrived and began rearranging furniture and lighting into the ambience of a passing. Setting out a dozen tables each with eight chairs covering both with matching white cloths, white crockery with gold trim and matching gold cutlery with a selection of glasses for each guest.

Nadia retired to her bedroom to prepare herself. She showered and dressed in the designer clothes purchased by her mother, and covered them over with her black abaya and hijab. She slipped on her low-heeled black designer shoes, leaving her face bare of make-up and fully moisturised. She inspected herself in the mirror and pondered.

I'm the perfect daughter for everyone to mourn. I won't tell them yet what I've done. I'll tell them after it's all over. Allah will show me the way forward but I'm still not getting any sign!

Mourners drove to the morgue to watch the body placed on a decorative stretcher enveloped in a shroud appear and gently guided into a private ambulance by Fatima's husband, sons and son-in-law.

All the men followed slowly behind the ambulance in their own cars as the immediate family with only three women: Nadia, Jamila and Huda joined the procession. The other female mourners proceeded back to Emirates Hills for the after-burial gathering.

Hidden Evil

It is discouraged for women to attend Islamic ceremonies but some families oblige their closest relatives and friends to attend. Nadia knew she could not accept unattendance of tradition and wanted to see her mother go into the earth in her final resting place.

The ceremony took place in the covered area next to a mosque where words to Allah were spoken by the Imam.

"Oh Allah, forgive Fatima Aktoum and elevate her station among those guided. Send her along the path of those who came before and forgive us and her. Oh Lord of the worlds, enlarge for hers, her grave and shed light upon her in it." He then silently delivered prayers as Nadia listened intently to scripture.

Oh Allah will you ever forgive my mother for her sins and mine too?

After prayers the mourners returned to their vehicles for the journey to the burial site. The stretcher was carried back into the ambulance by the same four relatives who gently carried it to the burial site upon arrival attended by all mourners.

The men placed stones inside the six-foot-deep hole to prevent the body from contacting with the soil and gently laid the body onto the top of them, with her right side facing Qibla. The men continued to place soil on the body until the grave was full.

Burial prayers were recited seven times by all mourners who placed their palms facing upwards until the grave was completely full of soil and patted down.

The women stood to the back of the mourners and

were not permitted at the immediate burial area or to engage in the ritual of placing soil on top of the body.

Nadia understood that her mother's body was in the ground and she would never see her or hear her again. She felt tense and trembled, her throat closed with dryness. She could not believe what she had done or how she would ever explain it to anyone.

Jamila and Huda placed their arms around her in comfort and to avoid her being noticed or her causing commotion by speaking or crying aloud, which was strictly forbidden during the burial.

If there's no body to detect foul play how can they tell. Please Allah give me a sign when to speak of my evil.

* * *

Afterwards at Emirates Hills, the men found the female mourners sitting in groups at the tables, leaving spaces in-between for them to join them after the burial. Everyone piled in to describe the wonderful ceremony fit for a wonderful god-fearing woman who had done so much for her family and their community.

"May she rest in peace with Allah," they echoed continuously.

Nadia sat numb at a table with her family listening to people's prayers, offering condolences and a new life for Fatima with Allah. Women showed emotion through quiet sobs, whilst men avoided the obligatory sharing of public emotion. The children were unconventionally quiet, knowing they should be.

Hidden Evil

Nadia had no tears or emotion to share as she took small bites of food with water to help melt it down her closed-up throat.

The mourners ate and drank the delights offered by the caterers, the maids helped serve the children to sugary Arabic delicacies and slowly moved around the room collecting dishes and plates along with the catering staff. Nadia felt nauseous and was sweating so decided to go to her bedroom to rest.

She arrived at the top of the stairs, at the exact spot where she had deliberately failed to grab her mother from falling.

Nadia stared down, seeing it happen again but this time more vividly and in slow motion.

I didn't do it deliberately. She slapped me and tried to slap me a second time, I was drunk but I still remember it all.

The vase of tulips crashed onto the floor and scattered everywhere in the scuffle and she slipped and lost her footing.

It wasn't my fault or hers it was an accident that she caused herself not me.

But the suffocation wasn't an accident, that was her willing me to do it!

Nadia slumped onto her bed fully clothed and fell asleep, away from the crowd chattering and noise downstairs. Feeling at peace before she closed her eyes.

Chapter Forty-Three

Nadia woke without memory and then it came flooding back that she had killed her mother. It was her 05.00 alarm. She was blissful after a resting sleep and, feeling excited, she went straight online and booked her one-way flight back to London.

She packed up her toiletries and the clothes she'd worn for the funeral into her already packed suitcase and went downstairs to make coffee before anyone woke.

The house is back to normal without a trace of a gathering the previous evening.

Did my mother die and get buried yesterday or was it all a dream?

I think I'm going mad and I know they'll put me back in that prison clinic if I confess to a murder I didn't commit.

This veil I have between truth and error is my intuition working overtime.

I'm getting out of here now and never coming back.

I don't want any memories of a hell house where the devil lives.

Nadia used the taxi app to take her to Emirates Airport.

The taxi arrived as she finished her hot sweet coffee. The driver greeted her with a smile and placed her suitcase into the boot of his car.

The drive to the airport was silent with few cars in sight. The lights inside the tall glitzy buildings of various architectural design shone through, gleaming different colours, some showing their individual interiors.

As she stared into buildings, she noticed people opening curtains and blinds ready to start their new day.

Each one of those people inside those apartments have their own story to tell. Are they all good people or have some committed atrocities and forgiven themselves? Will Allah forgive them, and me, on judgement day?

She checked in early for her flight and passed by Customs into the Emirates executive lounge to wait for her flight. She was two hours early for check-in but would rather be around strangers in an airport than be back at the mansion of hell.

* * *

She ate a hearty breakfast of eggs and avocado and drank mint tea. She decided to text Grace to say everything was fine and would call her later. She wanted to surprise Grace by turning up to see the look on her face as she entered their home.

The time arrived and she was on the plane sitting comfortably strapped in as it lifted into the skies towards London. Her heart raced and her hands began to sweat as she closed her eyes on take-off. She didn't like that part of any adventure.

After watching a movie and nibbling bits of food, she fell asleep and dreamed of Aisha, the woman with the knife from the clinic.

She was smiling with contentment as she glided away elevated from the ground and waving to Nadia robotically. Aisha had on her make-up, looking glamorous with a new bobbed shiny hairstyle wearing a long flowery maternity dress protruding full belly about to give birth.

"I'm better now, Nadia, my baby will be here soon," Aisha repeated in the dream.

At Heathrow airport Nadia weaved through the long line of passengers towards passport control then downstairs to pick up her baggage. She strode outside to the train to take her on to central London.

The sun shone on a beautiful spring day as the fresh air breathed with ease through her mouth and lungs. She stepped off the train at Hackney station. At the familiarity, she felt delighted to be almost home so she could hold Grace and Darcy in her arms again.

It was something she had previously taken for granted but had not had in her last few weeks of mental anguish, agony and physical torment at the clinic with electric shocks, straitjacket hand cuffed to the bed.

It was early afternoon and Grace would be home alone, Nadia didn't have her door keys with her so rang the bell on the Victorian glazed painted door, holding her breath.

I'm going to tell Grace what I've done because I can't keep a secret like this to myself. I'll go crazier keeping it all inside – it's not healthy for me!

'Oh my god, you're home!" Grace gushed as she grabbed Nadia into her arms and hugged her tightly.

Nadia reciprocated, thinking she must be in another dream. "I've never been happier to see you."

"You should've called me to pick you up. I've missed you so much."

"I wanted to surprise you after what I've put you through at hell mansion."

"Don't blame yourself. You didn't know what was planned for us. Let me put the kettle on and make some mint tea." Grace gently guided Nadia by the hand.

* * *

They sat down at the kitchen table and Grace began to notice a very different Nadia than the one she knew and loved but dismissed it.

"I have so much to tell you and ask about you too, I

don't know where to start," Grace said, placing her hand over Nadia's at the table.

"There's something I have to confess to you, Grace, but I don't know how to."

"You don't need to confess anything to me. Nothing's your fault. Don't you start blaming yourself for any of this when that monster abducted you in a helicopter and took you to the clinic." She was going to bang on the table, ready to explode again, but stopped after remembering that Nadia was also in mourning on top of her other distress.

"I need to tell you what evil I have done," Nadia said ignoring Grace's outburst.

"You're not the evil one, my love, that's your vile mother, not you. You need to get your head around what she's done to this family and stop thinking it's normal in any religion to commit such atrocities." Grace squeezed her hands over Nadia's.

"I killed her," Nadia said with her head down, eyes to the floor, pulling her hands out of Grace's grasp.

"What do you mean you killed her?" Grace spoke words she never imagined saying to anyone whilst staring towards Nadia, not wanting a response, and knowing that the clinic had far more severely damaged Nadia's mind than Grace had previously imagined or anticipated.

"I put my hand over her mouth and she stopped breathing in the hospital bed." Nadia put her head into her hands.

"What are you telling me? You've gone mad. No, you didn't kill your mother. You're grieving the shock of her death. There's no way you of all people could do such a thing. It's that clinic that's messed up your mind." Grace grabbed Nadia and hugged her tightly.

Nadia remained silent and offered no response to Grace's embrace.

"Listen, we'll get you professional therapy and get you back to your normal self again." Grace continued to embrace her tightly, refusing to let go.

"I killed her," Nadia repeated over and over as she collapsed onto the floor, breathing erratically.

"No, you didn't, Nadia. This isn't a confession, it's the shock of her death, coupled with the trauma that you've been through. Get onto your knees and put your hands onto the cold floor and breathe," Grace instructed firmly.

Grace sat on the floor on her knees next to Nadia holding her gently so she could breathe more easily. "You know your own mind you've got to stop thinking or talking like this."

"Maybe it was all a dream. I don't know what's real and what's not." Nadia replied gently as she breathed more easily and stood up to embrace Grace and accept that it must have all been part of the nightmare she had endured in the glittering city of Dubai.

Epilogue

"Hi Grace, how are you?" Nadia said cheerfully.

"I'm very happy to hear your voice. I'm recovering from clearing out some old tat but getting a grip on things. You sound cheerful. How are things going up there with Charlton?"

"Great thanks. He's perfect for what I needed and says I'm good to finish my sessions with him for now. So, I'll be home tomorrow. Can you pick me up at the train station?"

"Absolutely. What time?"

"I'll confirm later once I've booked my seat on the train. I'm so excited to see you both and be back at home away from this hotel."

"I'm ecstatic to know you're being discharged, after only two weeks with him. You're almost home and sounding like your old self again."

"Me too. I feel fabulous."

"Chat later. Bye now. Love you."

"I love you too. Bye."

THE END

Author's Note

At the date of publication, laws criminalising being gay remain a reality for one-third of countries worldwide.

Only eleven countries have banned conversion therapy, which is practised legally in countries that recognise equality.

It's still illegal in Brunei, Iran, Mauritania, Nigeria, Saudi Arabia and Yemen. These countries all impose the death penalty.

There are a further five countries where there is no legal certainty and the death penalty is a possibility. This is the case in United Arab Emirates, Qatar, Pakistan, Afghanistan and Somalia.

Russia have removed rights of equality.

Brazil have no laws against being gay but a gay person is murdered every thirty-six hours.

One in four adolescences have attempted suicide globally whilst coming to terms with their sexuality.

* * *

Author's Note

If you enjoyed reading this psychological thriller, please consider leaving a short review on Amazon. Your reviews are extremely appreciated, especially as I'm a self-published author and it helps other readers to decide if they would like to read it. Thank you.

Email: karenbradyauthor@gmail.com

Other Books by this Author

Agnes in Bloom – a Memoir

Acknowledgments

To my editor, Morgen Bailey, for being
(relatively) gentle with me.

Manufactured by Amazon.ca
Bolton, ON